THE
UNCOMMON
CURE

THE UNCOMMON CURE

A NOVELLA AND THREE STORIES

T. Agvanian

THE UNCOMMON CURE
A NOVELLA AND THREE STORIES

iUniverse books may be ordered through booksellers or by contacting:

iUniverse
1663 Liberty Drive
Bloomington, IN 47403
www.iuniverse.com
1-800-Authors (1-800-288-4677)

ISBN: 978-1-4917-7302-4 (sc)
ISBN: 978-1-4917-7301-7 (e)

Library of Congress Control Number: 2015912396

Print information available on the last page.

iUniverse rev. date: 9/29/2015

In memory of Nina and Vasgen

Contents

On Curing and Cooking

She understood that curing fish was a way of "cooking" it without the heat. Generally, the only ingredients required were salt and sugar. The rest—spices, alcohol, zest—were cosmetics and, like good makeup, brought out the natural beauty and taste of the original item by enhancing its intrinsic qualities. You could vary these extras, but you should never apply too much of any one in particular. This knowledge gave her comfort. Variety was the spice of life, and curing fish successfully could be achieved in a variety of ways and with a variety of spices.

While curing, she entertained herself by dreaming about the world. She thought the limitlessness of the cosmos was what made us believe in a supreme being, perform acts of love, have children, and write. Although she didn't realize it, she was dreaming about survival.

Her idea was to create an uncommon cure for fish by devising combinations of aromatic ingredients for purposes of achieving balance. She invented a Russian cure by drizzling vodka on the fish, a Jamaican cure with cinnamon and allspice berries, and a Mexican cure with tequila and cilantro, and she perfected the traditional Scandinavian cure with dill and cognac or aquavit. Naturally, some were more successful than others, but she enjoyed the exploration. She even thought of starting a small business until the smell of curing fish made her sick. When she reached a point of saturation, she decided this kind of business was not for her. In fact, any kind of business would not be for her. She was too much of a dreamer and not enough of a doer. Small organizations, she reasoned, were like big organizations in that any degree of success caused individuals at the pinnacles to believe less in chance and more in their own extraordinary qualities than was warranted by circumstance, and it caused individuals in the lower ranks to believe less in their extraordinary qualities and more in the determinism of chance than was warranted by circumstance. This, she felt, was true in politics as well. In some ways, it was consoling for her to witness time and again the immutability of human behavior. It gave her confidence that we were all members of the same species—designed by the same large, faraway hand—and within minor variations exhibited similar behaviors, such as envy, greed, pretense, generosity, and sometimes, even often, goodness of heart. She knew that at the end of the journey, whether we had commanded thousands, cured fish, written sonnets, composed symphonies, or studied the origins of the universe, we were destined for the same fate. We were like flavors; the stronger ones overwhelming the milder ones when combined, but deserving to be judged, at least in part, on the merits of how we would stand alone.

Long ago and far away, a much-cherished lover had offered her quality over quantity. She had meekly agreed to quality but then gotten neither. This was why such things ended. People did not always see eye to eye on what was important.

And everything changes. Love changes to hate or indifference. Hate often turns to indifference if one has not the stamina to fuel its unfriendly and consuming fires. Absolutely nothing stays the same, and we know this whether we study science or develop proofs, run a business, or simply lie awake at night, watching stars or listening to the person beside us breathe. Perhaps we seek an equilibrium in life and then labor to destroy it, or events beyond our control destroy it for us. As much as we try to create an order we can live with, the randomness of the external world grinds slowly—or not so slowly—to disrupt it. We cannot create comfort by dreaming it into existence, at least not forever. We can, however, escape temporarily into the life of an insular solitude to which no other has access. Madness, she concluded, *true madness, however, is a state of permanence.*

In any cooking or curing, sugar could behave as a counterpoint to salt. The objective was to achieve balance without resorting to force. But in her ruminations, she did not include dessert—despite her terrible sweet tooth—which she felt was governed by an alternative set of principles. The sugar should not be noticed, she reasoned, just as the salt should not be overwhelming. Her father had taught her to add sugar to cut the sourness of vinegar and the bitterness of certain spices. He also had shown her that the best-tasting meat stews were the result of adding fruits, such as dried apricots or figs, to a traditional base of fried onions and tomatoes. Every good cook knew that meats and fish were enriched by their exposure to opposites. The tongue, like the mind, was intrigued by mystery and bored by cloying sweetness. It recoiled at unrelenting bitterness.

She would eventually arrive at the most-ordinary conclusion: the way one behaved in life was determined in large part by an instinct to experience pleasure and to avoid pain, or at least to feel as little pain as possible. She would come to feel that freedom of choice was one of those mirages dreamed up by philosophers and theologians whose views of living were not cluttered by the mundane demands of practical survival; and to an extent, we humans would believe them. We would be inspired by pretty words and lofty thoughts, but we would be ruled by our fears, our traumas. It was the opposite of an inspiring thought, but it was true. *Think about it,* she would argue with herself. *We are guided by the light but driven by darkness.* This notion, of course, had been and would be infinitely disputed.

Sweet

We are incapable of not desiring truth and
happiness and incapable of possessing them.

—Pascal

Part I: Salt

Eva

Lavrentii walks me out to the porch. They call it a deck now. It is
screened in against insects and canopied around the edges to allow
salty air in while keeping the sun out. I am usually an early riser.
I've drunk some tea and eaten a whole-wheat cracker or two in
keeping with my modest regimen: eating foods low in carbohydrates
and sugars of any kind, natural or artificial, and eating more often
and in small quantities. Before leaving, Lavrentii asks me if I need
anything—a blanket for my knees perhaps, the required glass of
water, a pillow? I have my books and glasses. My open Turgenev
is arranged neatly on a small table next to my rocker. There is a
crocheted maroon afghan neatly folded on the back of my chair in
case I should feel a chill in the air or nod off to the sound of the
waves. All of the items are within easy reach. I am the picture-perfect

version of a contented senior citizen surrounded by a loving family while waiting for the light to fall. I tell him I am fine. He looks into my eyes, casually brushes away the heavy lock of black hair that obtrudes his vision, and kisses me on the cheek. "I'll be going out for groceries later," he tells me matter-of-factly. He will not ask me whether I need or would like anything from the local store, because he does not want an answer he cannot honor and wishes at all cost to avoid debates.

From here, there is a view of the ocean. It is early, and our neighbors are still asleep, or so it appears. I can barely see the house beyond the small rise, but the sharp sound of doors shutting can often be heard above the ocean's relentless rolling over this sand-and-pebble beach. Their daughter is Mercy's summertime friend, Maribel. I think Maribel is a pretty name. Mercy didn't come down for first breakfast this morning. Maybe she was up late, perhaps with Maribel or a book, or maybe she was attached to the gadget between her fingers, thumbs typing furiously with either a serious frown or a sly smile on her face. How delightful she appears to me when engrossed. Her expressions are a window into her thoughts—sometimes. She can keep secrets, I am sure—or am I romanticizing?

I can see Lavinia on a blanket, facing the ocean, with the still-comfortable sun coming up over the rocks in the distance. Soon she will begin her sun salutations, which she claims keep her calm and clear her head for the rest of the day. I enjoy watching this ritual. Her body has clean lines and tight limbs; it has no beehive folds along her back or crinkled thickness along her inner thighs. Her posterior is a little flat but still attractive. Mercy teases her when she compares the attributes of her own little bubble butt with her mother's. I understand why Lavrentii was drawn to Lavinia. From where I sit, she paints a striking picture with her straight blonde hair, which is brighter and more streaked, I think, in the summer. She wears it casually clipped to keep it from her face while she is greeting the morning. Although I cannot see her face, I imagine an expression of beatitude: eyes closed, a mere hint of happiness and

6

peace—Buddha as a work in progress. She warms up her muscles and joints by breathing deeply, rolling her neck and shoulders and then her hips, and twisting and folding her body until it is limber enough to withstand the rigorous contortions she will put it through to achieve harmony and calm. I must confess it is a pleasure to watch. Like a dancer, she makes it look effortless, and her movements have a natural grace. I am glad it is so, if only for Mercy's sake. I am no mercenary, but I understand the market.

Every day I think something will change. She will confer with Lavrentii and decide I shall be allowed to eat anything I want. It would be less of a headache for her and less heartache for everyone else. It is time for me to enjoy the precious little time I have with my grandchild, my meandering thoughts, and my culinary indulgences and to make peace with my conscience. Besides, when I am gone, they will mourn for me a short time, and in private, they will sigh that they have been relieved of their burden. Yes, they will say dutifully, "We did everything we could for her. The ordeal is over; she is at peace." And they will be praised by fine friends, professional and otherwise, for their fortitude and perseverance in caring for that "old woman," whom they will call difficult, impossible, or even crazy under their breath. It's just as well for me. There are no others who will bemoan my passing or think me gone too early or too good. Only Branka will remember me as I wish to be remembered, but she too will not last long. That's life: long when you are in its prime and short when it is effectively over. So it will be—I guarantee it. Soon.

Instead, we are destined to repeat our daily comedy. It's time for Lavinia to return from her precious salutations. After neatly rolling up her blanket and stuffing it into a red cylindrical bag, Lavinia begins her leisurely ascent back to our cottage. Her feet drag along the way. Perhaps she wishes to appear carefree, released from tiresome worries, and ready for the day's labors. She looks up at me, hesitates for a moment or two, and then waves. "Good morning, Eva!" she calls out. Today I pretend to be engrossed in my reading. Yet she knows I am watching. I can hear the sliding door open into her bedroom. Lavrentii must be out somewhere, for there is no telltale sound of voices or sweet whisperings. Yes, I'm ancient, but my hearing is acute. She quickly showers, performs her ablutions, and enters my space.

"What will it be today—an egg, some sausages, toast?" she asks.

Without looking up from my book, I answer, as always, agreeably. "I'll have whatever you're having." I know that it doesn't matter what I want but what she deems acceptable that will find its way to my late-breakfast menu. Of course there will be kiwi on that menu. *Damned kiwi. Again.* When she leaves, I look out at the vast ocean. The sun is higher now. I gaze at the spot where she performed her morning stretches, and I feel an absence has painted itself into this picture. The morning is returning its greeting, but there is no one on this side to accept the salutation.

Again, I hear bathroom sounds from the other side of the house—the flush of the toilet, running water. Mercy is brushing her teeth while she sings with the voice of an angel. The notes are delivered with childlike messiness between irregular gargles and random squirts. I can see her in my mind's eye, dancing to an inaudible rhythm that propels her small backside, her bubble butt, in many different directions at once. She is still young—thirteen on her last birthday—but on the verge, a blossom ready to burst on the world. Perhaps the sounds are strung together in her mind's hearing. I don't recognize the song. But why should I, a prehistoric crone like me? Mercy will soon be ready for breakfast. Perhaps I will join them, if only for the company. There is nothing more for me between now and lunchtime.

* * *

"Eva, please put that spoon down." "Ee-va" she calls me. Her admonition carries the mere hint of a controlled stridency that dwells just below the natural timbre of her voice.

Lavinia appears stricken again, as if mortally wounded while performing an act of goodwill. Although I do not acknowledge her, I gently lay the spoon on the table and wipe my mouth with the dinner napkin. "Imbecile," I whisper under my breath. She notices my head bobbing with indignation but not the slight additional tremor in fingers already tremulous with age.

"I beg your pardon?"

Lavrentii's wife takes a deep breath and then carefully considers her aim. The endless, silent sigh follows. I watch her demurely from the corner of my eye. Such a model of probity am I that I would not recognize myself in the mirror. I might as well don a mustache. Lavrentii, in silent repose, is the picture of a long-suffering Russian monk about to pray, hands folded against his forehead. I know from his childhood habit that his eyes are closed as he steels himself for what is yet to come. Lavinia is in modified combat stance, preparing to do battle with her ill-behaved mother-in-law. Her weapons are firm righteousness and unchallenged medical omniscience. Dr. Lavinia knows best. I must appreciate that she has only my best interests at heart. I believe this to be true. She is used to molding the rational world into any shape she desires. Her successes prove that it can be done, and they have delivered her a great measure of professional self-confidence. Brava! This is how it usually goes when she shares her medical anecdotes.

"How could they have been such fools?" she says, laughing, when she describes her interns. She is the star of her own stories—a supernova surrounded by white dwarves. Since I have been in this predicament, I have often wondered how they found each other— Dr. Lavinia and Dr. Lawrence, in that order. They could not be more different: he is intuitive, perceptive by nature, and even mystical, like some of the religions he studies, and she is fiercely scientific, as rational as a slide rule. Poor, gentle Lavrentii, dubbed Lawrence for American audiences. No simpleton he, but a bumpkin nevertheless. Was he snared by a conniving doctor of neurophysiology, whatever that is, or dazzled by an intelligence with a lovely face? I try to preempt an outright burst of the lady's vehemence, but I am not altogether successful.

I smile. "I wanted only to taste it. How much would that have harmed?"

"Eva, we made the other pudding for you." Lavinia's voice cracks. "Lance, can you try to reason with her?"

"Mother, you understand—I know you do—that if we can keep your blood sugar under control, you won't have those dizzy spells."

Lavrentii's voice is pleading, his tone reasonable with a dash of exasperation. Poor, dear Lavrentii. There is no spark of wildness or mystery in him anymore. He seems obedient and dutiful. If he could only relax. I am certain he has taken a better measure of these events than she, with her formulas and medical equations. I remember when he first brought her home to meet us. Lavrentii Sr. was still alive. She was as pink and smooth as a peach and had nearly flaxen hair. She was lovely, actually, and charming, almost obsequious when they were courting. She gushed, plying me with compliments whenever I made my lox. "Yes, I learned how to cure it at home," I explained. "In fact, I experimented with many cures and finally settled on one of my own invention—a sort of cross between Scandinavian and Slavic. Instead of using cognac, I drizzled the salmon with the finest, most-aromatic slivovitz I could find." She never cajoled me into revealing my secret ingredient. She didn't care enough, although she ate it with great gusto. The secret is dried orange peel, if you must know. It absorbs some of the fishiness. But that is neither here nor there.

In any case, she helped me with the cooking and cleaning. I told her I hated bringing maids into the house. I was getting old, after all. "Can't stand a stranger touching my personals. Branka's all right, though. Branka is different. Branka I have known for over sixty-five years. Branka is too old now to help me clean, but I like her company," I told them again after Lavrentii Sr. died and they offered to hire me a housecleaner.

In those days, Lavinia wanted desperately to be a friend to her mother-in-law, to cultivate an understanding. "We have an understanding," she would say with a laugh when Lavrentii and his father stumbled into the kitchen while we—I mean I—prepared dinner. She watched, pretending to learn, pretending female collusion. She thought she was fated by her name to be part of this family. "What a coincidence!" she squealed at the combination.

It was not much of a coincidence as far as I could see. *Two Ls. Und?* I thought, as the Germans would say. Of course, we laughed, but I felt at first it was a bit stupid, even immature. I sensed that there were gaps in her emotional development. *Could it be that she is a well-educated dope?* I thought then. That's what they said about Winifred Wagner, patron of opera and admirer of Hitler. I don't mean to suggest the politics of a troglodyte, to be sure—more like the Cleavengers of the world, academic upstarts without an iota of common sense, capable only of formulaic responses, at best, to the most vexing of human problems. Like mine. Like me. Yes, we were all taken in by stories of her vast accomplishments. In all fairness to her accomplishments, she has indeed come a long way from where she started. This I have intuited through shreds of information dropped inadvertently and squelched just as suddenly. I knew she would be a welcome addition to the gene pool, a virtual guarantee of talented and intelligent grandchildren. On that score, if on no other, I reasoned wisely. And she seemed to make Lavrentii happy. Besides, what did I have to say about it? Again, in fairness, she has tried exceptionally to fit into this odd family with its arcane history, its feet in two continents and its head in another. It cannot have been easy for her. After the initial patina of her gifts wore off, I felt she didn't give a fig about Lavrentii's mother or father. Once she had tightened her talons around his throat, she flew off with the smitten boy and left Lavrentii Sr. and me alone to bicker and to age. Without Lavrentii, we festered and began to rot. Now he's back, and she's back with him. Lavrentii no longer comes without a price. We get the package deal: Mrs. Doctor Neurophysiology and company.

"I used to make crème caramel from scratch for Lavrentii's father. I was curious how yours measured up to mine," I say. I am the model of diffidence. Every day I have kiwi or an orange for dessert. I am sick to death of kiwis and oranges. Why do they devour crème caramel in front of me if they expect me to behave? I'm surrounded by *ooh*s and *yum*s, paroxysms of ecstasy over some sugar and eggs. I don't mind, really. *But give me a piece of the tart!*

She thinks I don't notice when she sighs despairingly, or she doesn't care. She looks at Lavrentii again, as if to say, "Your mother." Do I detect another message exchange? I see an ever-so-slight rolling of the eyes. I am a misbehaving specimen again. Even chimpanzees are treated better than old folks like me, marginalized primates dribbling saliva into napkins tucked into their collars. They don't know what's best for them. Daughter-in-law knows best. I turn beseechingly to Lavrentii. Like a small child, Lavrentii looks down again. Any second now, I expect his head to drop onto his plate. He knows I'll notice the collusion behind swapping eyes.

Lavrentii Sr. was a sweet man too, and he adored me. I suppose what passed between us was love, our particular brand of love—except toward the end, when he would routinely raise his cane and accuse me of adultery after fifty years of marriage. *Old fool.* Even today, I cannot imagine what was going through his mind. At the end, he was like a child. He cried at the slightest provocation—when he wasn't threatening to beat me with his cane, that is. He claimed I had been unfaithful. He couldn't know that to be true—unless he could see into my head.

They say you should never judge a person by his or her relatives. Mine are all dead except for my son and granddaughter. My daughter-in-law doesn't count.

We have been here for nearly a week. It was Lavrentii's idea, I suspect, although she tried to take credit. She, biblical in her ambition, might have thought that through sheer will and reason, she could cure me of my illness and raise me from the nearly dead, so to speak. "A couple of weeks of rest and relaxation near the water. Together," she reassured me in her most doctor-ly voice.

The entire family is here—or what is left of it. The only one who matters to me is Mercy. The other two have come here to fornicate in the dark to the sound of the ocean and to soothe each other's conscience before I die.

Mercy

"Babushka, when did you meet Joseph?"

Mercy walks me to my room, where the bed has been made by invisible fingers, and helps me to lean into pillows she has propped against the headboard. The bed stands flush with the corner in case I lean too far and tip myself over. What a perfect painting that would make. Ha! She places another more-compact pillow into that corner for my elbow to rest on. I am stretched on a diagonal, allowing space for her to sit facing me. I have a light summer throw over my knees, but my multicolored toes are exposed. They seem to fascinate rather than disgust the clinically minded child. It must be something she gets from her mother. The light from the window envelops her face and her bronzed knees, which she has lifted to the footboard. She leans forward to examine tiny pustules on the skin of her legs or pulls at the silken hairs while she talks and listens. I abruptly grasp her hands together and bring them to my lips for a kiss. They tickle my bulbous olfactory organ with the perfume of ocean, commercial sunblock, and fresh air. This is how the beginnings of life must have smelled churning together in a primordial soup without labels.

"Josip, *Golubka*. Josip." I gently correct her pronunciation: "Yoh-sip."

Mercy looks like me—a little bit anyway. She looks as I did when I was young, that is. She has deep, almond-shaped brown eyes like her father's, ergo like mine, and her hair tends toward the dark of our family. She looks more like Lavrentii than Lavinia. That is my opinion anyway. When Lavrentii makes light of their similarities, as he did this morning—"You sound just like your mother when you're describing the shells you've collected, all scientific and such"—I keep my mouth shut. She comes to my room every day after breakfast to hear my stories. Why shouldn't I tell her how Josip used to write me letters in that delicious, no-frills Cyrillic of his? His letters were short but suggestive. I recall his handwriting was neat but had a tremulous, uneven quality to it. I cannot understand how people communicate through electronic mail. You might as well lick the TV. Letters are palpable and personal. You can see immediately from the handwriting if the message comes from the heart.

"I was a few years older than you are now when I first saw him in the market. His mother sold fruits and vegetables. When I stepped up to buy some, he pretended not to notice me." I am playing the old coquette to my granddaughter's innocence. "His mother wiped her hands on her apron just before she smacked him on the side of his head, and then he offered me apples and pears. But he couldn't look me in the eye at first."

Mercy is amused. Her black eyes widen. "Oh, Grandmama."

"It was just a way of getting his attention. Once, later, when I had become a regular customer, he produced a pomegranate. I didn't know what it was and bit into it as if it were an apple. He laughed. Gave me a cloth to wipe the juice from my chin. Then he broke it open for me. I wanted to suck the sweet, tart liquid from his fingers. But when I saw his mother watching him watching me, I became afraid she would poke him again. My mother asked me later what the red spots on my blouse were. I told her about the boy at the market and the pomegranate. The spots left a permanent stain."

"What did she say when you told her?"

"I lied. At that time, it was a forbidden thing."

"To eat pomegranates?"

"No, silly."

"For you to know a boy in the market?"

"My little innocent. No. No. No. For both of us. For people of different faiths. His people didn't trust us, and mine didn't like his. We were so different—that's all."

"Is that why it was forbidden? Because you were so different?"

"But Josip and I were not different at all. We were cut from the same cloth."

"You said 'forbidden' before."

"Not forbidden so much as less practiced. His people considered us to be ignorant peasants who could barely read or write. We considered them intruders foreign in the way they looked, dressed, and spoke and, more important, in the way they worshipped. Any fraternization between the sexes was frowned upon." Mercy puzzles over the phrase "fraternization between the sexes" and is perhaps then titillated by the suggestion of salacious things to come. I continue. "Though it happened often enough, it was always noted. By the middle-aged women mostly—the vipers and the wags. The young ones and the very old ones didn't care so much."

"Did your mother worry about you?"

"She once said, 'If this is your destiny …,' but he was afraid because of his father or maybe his faith. We even planned to run away together."

"You did? Who? You mean Josip?" Her eyes widen, and her nose wrinkles as if the picture of a decrepit old woman running away with a young boy is too difficult to conjure. I am in a reclining position. One of the pillows has slipped below my hip, and I am no longer upright. Mercy notices my discomfort. As she gently attempts to straighten the pillows behind me, her face brushes against mine, and I use the opportunity to plant a quick kiss on her forehead. I breathe in another whiff of her breakfast breath. Her skin is smooth, and I can smell the Ivory from this morning's washing. I notice the delicate wisps of hair at her temples embracing features that will soon shed their childhood adipose. Her silken dark hair is pulled up in a ponytail.

"Why don't you let me braid your hair the way we did in Russia?" I remind her of the photograph in the living room, taken of me in a displaced-persons camp in Germany after the war. They call them French braids for some reason—the French are always taking credit. The braids frame my face and are tied at the back. One cannot see the ribbon in the picture.

"Your hair was so beautiful. Did you streak it then, Grandmama?"

"Of course not, *Tzvetochek*, my little flower. The sun always made the tops look lighter. Yours on top is lighter too. The braiding weaves the darker layers of hair from below with the brighter ones above. Let me try."

She undoes her hair and shakes it out. Again, the sweet, clean, fruit-like scent reaches me. I would like to bury my face in her fragrant innocence. She combs her hair with her fingers. It is heavy and falls evenly to her shoulders. I begin to work the layers uniformly from her temples. She bends her neck to endure more easily the discomfort. How well her hair cooperates. *Perhaps love, like genes, skips generations, or maybe we can love only the innocent,* I think while I braid, trying to absorb the inebriating smell of youth.

"Babushka, did you run away with Josip?" This time, she pronounces his name right.

I work slowly, nudging her head gently in my direction. "We ran away on our bicycles. But we didn't ride very far."

* * *

It is Abraham's moon, a tryst of fate. There is a tap at the partially open window. I am ready. It's good that it is springtime. Or is it early summer? I don't need much clothing.

He has attempted a crude disguise—he has wrapped a cloth around his mouth. I'm sure I could recognize his lashes in the darkness. He removes a pastry from his pocket, opens my fingers, and places it in my hand. It contains walnuts, sugar, and a spice I do not recognize, wrapped in buttery dough. It smells heavenly, piquant. I bite into it. When I offer him the rest, he whispers, "For you. *Davai*. Let us ride." The window cooperates silently. I need to slide it up slightly to pass through. He has left his cycle at the side of the road. When I am out, we embrace. I recognize in his mouth the sweet pungency that I have just eaten. He tells me there are more pastries in his bag at the side of the road. I must lift my bicycle, which I parked conveniently behind the house, by the back door, to prevent the creak of gears from waking my mother. He helps me carry it away from the house. I have taken nothing but a light sweater and a change of underwear.

We ride for an hour or more before stopping for relief. The only sounds are the whirring of the wheels, the occasional stone, and the crickets, whose chirping is past before we can perceive it. Even the sleeping dogs have no interest in our escapade. They ignore us as we ride. How long do we ride—an hour, two? Much more or much less? We have hardly spoken. When he motions for me to stop, I obey. He is looking for something—a marker perhaps. I follow as he walks his bicycle into the woods. He lifts it and grasps the wheels to silence the sound of the bike's primitive gears. I do the same, although for me, the task is more demanding, and I must struggle to keep up and remain quiet while moving. He seems to know this place. We walk for several minutes in the dead of night before we are in a small hollow large enough for us and our cycles. I notice that inside, the music of the night has been blunted, and we seem to be alone in the universe. He has brought a light covering, which we place on the dank earth redolent of mushrooms and decaying leaves. As we lie together, I am not aware of the rocks and smaller stones that will leave temporary marks in my skin. It is a wonder that I remember them now. Or am I fabricating details that my mind has chosen to ignore for over half a century? When we make love for the first time, I do not understand that the wetness flowing between us is of coupling and blood. We lie exhausted yet acutely alert to every sensation of touch and the muted sounds of the forest.

The apocalypse is about to erupt, though we know nothing of it. We are mere children.

"I want to smell you and taste you," I tell him. He places a finger to my lips, as if there is danger. I hold his hand to my mouth and kiss it gently. It exudes sweetness from a wonder spice I later learn to be cinnamon mixed with the acrid pungency of our desperate lovemaking. We feel we have been riding for a lifetime, and either from fear or joy, we are overcome by weariness. Blackness covers us like a blanket.

* * *

"Where did you go, Babushka?"

"Nowhere," I tell her matter-of-factly. "We rode for an hour or so, and then we turned back." She turns to look at me. She is puzzled. I resume the braiding on the other side. "We had no plan. He was afraid."

"Weren't you afraid too?"

"Maybe. I don't remember anymore about fear or trepidation or danger or anything. When we were riding, I didn't care about my mother or father or brother—or anything else in the world, for that matter. Now, here at my age, the heart beats only for pleasure, and you are my pleasure, *Tzvetochek.* But I can still taste the pastry. You call it *rugallah,* I think. Then I didn't know anything as wonderful as cinnamon existed."

"I love cinnamon too. My favorite are cinnamon buns." She seems overjoyed that we have this in common. I fear she has a sweet tooth. The generations are odd. Lavrentii preferred pickled things, especially vinegar pickles, half-sours like the ones we made in Russia. He adored ripe red tomatoes in brine. He never ate dessert unless he was ordered to. Imagine ordering a child to eat his chocolate! He was a strange child. But she is like me. She loves sweets and chocolates and licks the frosting on cake, even when it is the common variety without much nuance. American birthday cakes are an abomination.

I believe she will become more sophisticated about desserts as she ages. It must skip generations—this sickness, this craving. I see she likes thinking about sweet foods, perhaps because I have seen them rationed by the enforcer.

"One piece only," Lavinia tells her. Do I notice a slight nick of the child's shoulders, as if she is secretly wishing for a cookie, as I am?

"Do you think your parents will indulge an old lady in cinnamon toast?" I blurt the words out. Suddenly, it occurs to me that I can collude with my granddaughter for some old-fashioned cookies. I'm famished again and crave sugar and cinnamon. I watch, hungry, not only for sweets but also for a sign. Surely this lovely creature will take pity upon an old hag in her desperation.

Mercy wants to get back to the story. "Grandma, what happened then? Were you mad at him?"

"Darling, today, over sixty years later, I'm still mad at him. Sometimes it is just one step, one turn, one retreat that pushes you in a direction that will alter the course of your life completely." I hesitate. I do not wish to confuse her—or wound her if she understands. "But then I wouldn't have you. So maybe it is all for the best. We don't understand the master plan, do we?" I look into her eyes to see if the words have reached their intended target. I am sincere, am I not? But I want to return to the matter at hand: my toast.

"Grandmother?" She looks me straight in the eye and sits up like a dancer about to leap, her tone shifting to formal. She hesitates but then proceeds, a serious schoolgirl asking the teacher an impertinent question. As she gently removes the wisps of disobedient curls from her face, she runs her hand along the braid I have woven. Her fingers dwell on the braid's contours as she assesses the feel of it against her scalp. She says it is a little tight, but I think she is content with the new hairstyle. Her long fingers are well defined, clean from the ocean. The fingernails are cut short. "Do you believe in God?"

I am taken aback by the question. My ulterior interest in matters concerning cinnamon toast has been usurped by philosophy—or, better yet, religion. What does God have to do with sugar? I see by her expression she will not be deflected. When did she begin to wonder if there is more to it all than nice hair and great flavors? I prayed in church when I was young. I loved the smells of incense, of smoke, but I don't remember feeling insignificant until much later, after the war had jabbed a stake through my once-modest ambitions. I'm like Dracula—dead but walking around in sunshine, smelling freshness, youth, and innocence and plotting to use the one I love most in this world to get some cinnamon toast, a sweet carbohydrate. The toast will be anathema to the system but ambrosia for the heart.

"I believe there are things we cannot know in this life, no matter how much we hope and dream that there is more beyond it. Sometimes we pretend to be philosophers and appear to make decisions out of principle. We act—or not—out of what we perceive as honor or faith. But in fact, oftentimes, we are just swept along by history or by our feelings. We seek to excuse our behavior by whatever creed is convenient." I am afraid this explanation is too much for my thirteen-year-old granddaughter. I cannot deprive her of a childhood by filling her head with confusing philosophies. Suddenly, I am overcome with a love I cannot fully fathom for this child, whom I wish to protect, embrace, and cover with soft, elderly kisses. I want to warn her of impending danger and shield her against the bitterness of disappointment that must come sooner or later. She looks at me boldly. I don't think she is afraid to ask. Perhaps she understands more than she cares to express.

My first husband, Panas, used to say that if you had food and sex, you didn't need religion. He believed that all people in the world want to do is eat, make love, and work gainfully. When he talked like that, I reminded him that we are creatures of imagination as well. We are capable of dramatic fictions to excuse our misery. Those fictions propel us forward and backward, in directions progressive and lethal. Isn't the history of the last century, of any century, the march of uncertain fictions? Isn't life a historical catalogue of decisions made in the hope of finding not just safety or happiness but also pure joy? Isn't hope the product of our dreams?

"Babushka, what happened to Josip?" Mercy is pulling me back to earth again.

"I think his father boxed his ears but not too harshly. I'm sure they were glad to get him back. He had betrayed their faith by running off with a *goy*." I expect her to ask me about the term *goy*, but she refrains. I'm surprised she knows the word. "But my father—he slapped me just once without a question or word. I was terrified because his hand shook, and I was afraid he would pick me up and throw me against the wall. Today they call that abuse, but in Russia, it was discipline. My face hurt for days. My mother hardly spoke to me. Even when she brought me kasha, she couldn't bear to look at me."

"Did you hate him?"

"Whom? My father?"

"Him too. I meant Josip."

"No. Neither."

"Where did Josip go after you got back?"

"I was angry with Josip." After all these years, I have to get this off my chest. Suddenly, the memory of the pungent smell of cinnamon brings on a nineteenth-century-like swoon, causing me to fall back into my pillow, which has slipped again. I hit the walnut headboard hard, but I shrug off the pain. "He threw it all away in one moment of indecision. I would have lived to die for him and with him, if necessary." I sound melodramatic. Why can't I just tell her a cloying fairy tale? This is America. She looks me straight in the eye, unwavering. She is shocked perhaps by this sudden outburst from a wheezing, cantankerous, diabetic, wrinkled old bat whose only pleasure of late is sugar and whom she calls *Babushka*. She's probably wondering how this old lady was capable of such powerful feelings. It is beyond the young to imagine that we were ever like them. I too am surprised that a hurt inflicted well over half a century ago can raise my blood pressure today. *Okh, okh, okh, chevo ya malenkim ne zdokh. Okh, okh okh, why didn't I croak as a child?*

* * *

When I open my eyes, I can see the shafts of light streaming into our hollow. I think it is time to go, and I am ready. Josip is standing above me and looking down, weeping. I lift my hand to him. He takes it but remains still, resisting. *"Ne mogu,"* he says, blubbering like the child he still is. "I can't."

* * *

I partially close my eyes, pretending stillness, wishing for sleep. I expect Mercy to leave me, but instead, she sits and watches, as if wondering whether I am faking it. Her eyes wander to the foot of my bed and rest on my feet, especially my gnarled and misshapen toes. The middle one on my left foot is missing. I would expect her to be repulsed by the sight of corrupted flesh. Instead, she draws closer, as if she wishes to examine it. Her face is so near that I can feel her breath on my foot. I am certain she can smell the decay. She touches the big toe of my left foot with her index finger as if it is an insect not yet dead. I drift off for only a moment, I think. When I open my eyes again, she is gone.

Mercy, Mercedes, my flower, my grace.

* * *

It is another day, another morning. Breakfast comes and goes without incident. The table has been set for early lunch with bright-colored napkins and blue plates. Everything has been arranged to greet the morning with a smile. Mercy, my little mermaid, is wearing her blue bathing suit with yellow stripes. She has not undone the French braid. Lavrentii stops whistling an Italian melody—from *La Traviata*, I think—to plant a kiss on his daughter's forehead.

"Mmmm. You smell like watermelon. You're up early, aren't you?" He catches himself, but it is too late. I have a momentary vision of bathing in fruit salad chock full of watermelon—without kiwi or oranges.

I think, *What an old* baba *I am. Ha.*

Lavinia bustles about, arranging the bread and jam. Although they have not yet made their appearance at the table, I can see the kiwi and oranges on the counter. She appears unusually chipper today.

I have submitted to my shot without complaint. They let me eat bread. It is about time. I pretend to be grateful. Today it is a small piece of *boule* with Gruyère and one hard-boiled egg. I like a little anchovy paste on my egg. She passes it to me and smiles as if doling out indulgences, tickets to heaven for sinners. She knows I like Gruyère and Appenzeller and usually makes them available— but not before feigning outrage at their "prohibitive expense," as she calls it. If she could cut out the bread, she would. What would life be without a thick piece of sourdough with a slab of unsalted butter? *Khleb c maslom.* But I am allowed only one piece. I drink my coffee with artificial sweetener as I masticate the *boule* seven times on each side, like a mechanical old cow with a rotating jaw—first left and then right. I smile at Mercy, not wishing to appear insincere. Lavrentii wants to peal me a kiwi, but I assure him I am not yet an invalid. They laugh at my good humor. *Ha-ha.* They congratulate themselves for my good fortune, content to believe that I am making progress. "Your blood sugar was excellent this morning." It is Lavinia again. She feels my blood-sugar level is her personal accomplishment. When she smiles, it is only with her mouth. Her eyes are like blue granite. No crow's-feet have formed around the corners.

Lavrentii begins to clear the plates.

"Babushka, will you tell me more about Josip?"

"I don't know how much I can remember."

"Who is Josip?" Lavinia turns toward Mercy.

"Yes, Merc, who is Josip?" Lavrentii pronounces Josip's name correctly.

"It is *our* secret." I preempt Mercy's response, careful to maintain a gregarious manner. We are like two little girls, giggling in harmless collusion.

"Is Babushka teaching you some Russian?" Lavinia is hopeful.

"*Da.*" Mercy, I understand, has suddenly become my ally.

Mercy, finished with her irregular nibbling, is now gathering her things: a book she is reading, Robert Cormier's *I Am the Cheese*; a tube of sunblock, number 15; and her red tennis towel. She slips her bare feet into her thongs, walks over to me, kisses me on the cheek, and tells me she will see me later. For a moment, I can smell the sand and salt left over from yesterday's swim. I am suddenly overcome with the desire to lick the flavors of the ocean from her luminescent cheeks and her eyelashes and hair.

Imagine this at my age.

* * *

Branka once told me that when you come into this world, you pick the parents you get, because you need to learn something in this life that you have overlooked in the last one.

"A lesson about forgiveness or about loyalty or faith. The parents you choose teach you to endure hardship, resist temptation, or submit to God." She is always submitting to the will of her creator. I usually indulge her because she is kind and religious in a way that does not pass for barter.

"When I die, I want my children to dig a hole in the backyard—deep—and bury me in that hole," I say.

Branka laughs because she thinks I am joking. Branka is a Slav but believes, so far as I can tell, that between lives, we float in an alphabet soup of intelligence and light—pure understanding. Then we volunteer for further duty with a map of obstacles to be surmounted, like an endless road and a game in which we get to choose our shelter and weapons. "Branka," I say with a laugh, "what lessons has my child learned from me? How to be an American gentleman with a puffed-up nickname? He certainly hasn't learned to choose his women wisely."

"But you see how your grandchild has turned out. She is *her* daughter too."

I am silenced by her leaps of faith.

* * *

Both of my parents were as hard as diamonds, but neither was as beautiful. I have been thinking about such things while fantasizing about fresh summer watermelon. I saw Lavrentii carrying one in from the car. I wonder if the good doctor will offer it to me or eat it in secret. It is kiwi and oranges every day for me. *Save me,* Gospodi, *from another day of kiwi and oranges.*

* * *

You first make one plan and then another—"*und beide tut man nicht,*" as the song tells us—and you do neither. Destiny has a way of destroying our best intentions.

We could hear the shooting at the edge of the village, and we knew.

I was seventeen when the Germans shipped us off to work in their munitions factories. They called us *Ostarbeiter*. We sat in trucks on the way to Germany, listening to the soldiers singing songs about their *heimat*. Some behaved kindly toward us. We were barely younger than some of them, and the ones who smiled back hadn't yet learned that in the new order—a brave, new world cleansed of impurities—we Slavs were to become the servants and the workers. Fraternization had not yet become a crime. Without their uniforms, some of them were just misguided and obedient boys. I can say that only now, understanding that children with deadly weapons are a terrifying sight. At the time, I must have been confused and no less preoccupied.

My father stayed away on that morning. After the escapade with Josip, he barely spoke to me. For an eternity, I was certain he took no further interest in my fate, but I now believe he was ashamed of the black eye he gave me or perhaps of more villainous deeds I cannot bear to imagine. A self-made, semicultured semibrute of a man who loved writing, words, and books in a village full of brutes did not have the strength to say good-bye. My mother, on the other hand, came to the gathering and watched me climb aboard. When we embraced for the last time, she didn't say a word but held me so hard I could barely catch my breath. Through my sobs, I noticed the ring of grime embedded in the folds of her neck and struggled in my attempt to wipe it away with my thumb and forefinger. I still remember the slightly acrid smell of her perspiration. When they pulled us apart, she remained standing like a statue in a rainstorm—stiff, bedraggled, weather-beaten, and disregarded. I wonder if she guessed that she would never see me again. She had a habit of tearing her cuticles with her fingers when she worried. I had once seen her nearly destroy the index finger and thumb on her left hand, when my brother lay in a fever from which they thought he would not recover. But he did. And now I could see her hand bleed as she wiped it on her apron. I imagined her sobbing face as I was hoisted into the truck. But when I turned, I saw that her eyes were dry, vacant. Among all of the wailing mothers, she was the one dry-eyed exception. Later, I learned from a cousin that it was months before she spoke in sentences again. But on that cold October morning, she could not easily have borne the sight of my departure. By the time I had found a spot in the corner of the transport, she had run back into the house. I managed to catch a glimpse of her black woolen skirt as she closed the door.

Il'ko, my brother, died fighting.

At first, the people in the village thought the advancing Germans would save them from one fierce monster and his devastating

26

five-year plans. As the tanks and trucks rolled into the village square, the mayor and his cohorts welcomed the Germans with bread and butter and eggs. Soon they complied peacefully with the Germans' demands that the families donate one healthy young person to the war effort. The Germans accepted their gifts, dismissed them, and soon got down to their dirty business. It did not take long to understand the nature of the new beast in town. My lovely young brother, Il'ko, understood it immediately. He was gone in a flash.

Even before the Germans arrived, we had been living in hell. It was a time of shifting alliances, denunciations, and severe want, when small people struggled to save themselves. My father knew a man, a shopkeeper, who had been denounced by someone in the village for plotting against the life of the leader. This man had a wife and two young children. For over a year, this man—an Armenian or maybe a Georgian, an other in our Slavic satellite state—sat in a Soviet jail, refusing to sign a confession. After a year of refusals, he was released without explanation. By that time, his store was gone, along with his livelihood, and he was conscripted into the Soviet army to fight the Germans, who had made deep incursions into the Ukraine. It was no wonder that this other eventually became a German prisoner of war. It was said that he hid in a hole until it was safe to surrender, because he feared being shot by his own side more than being shot by the enemy. Perhaps he felt he would get a better deal with the invaders. Everyone was looking for a better deal in those times. There were none to be had.

No one really knew who the enemy was. During the preventable hunger of '33, Mother made *kotletki* from tree bark instead of meat and grain because the grain had been confiscated for the big cities. It was vile, bitter frenzy food. People dropped dead in the streets. Il'ko had eaten rotting horse flesh and lapsed into fever. Mother kept a night vigil, bathing his body, cooling it with a paste of cool yogurt, and praying for a break in temperature. For three days, we watched and waited. On the third day, he got up, put on his clothes, and marched out of the house. For the sake of his personal legacy, Il'ko was lucky enough to pick the right enemy. I cannot say the same for my father, at least not for certain. The other enemy of this war, our own personal bogeyman, coddled by the Western powers because he played his cards better, joined the winning side and prevailed.

The last time I saw Josip in Russia, he again came to my window at night. I didn't want to talk to him. I was angry that he had abandoned me in the forest. He was the reason for my black eye. I thought he had come to apologize.

"Why did you turn and run from me?" I asked him again, still seeing my abject figure running after him as he rode away, back in the direction of the town. I cannot remember what went through my mind as I sat exhausted at the side of the road, gasping in disbelief at the sound of the roosters crowing in the distance. How small the universe of a child is. He tapped several times before I acknowledged him.

"I've come to say good-bye," he said.

"Josip, do not leave. I have never stopped thinking about you," I managed to whisper.

"I cannot stay. It is not safe for us here. Please let me kiss you one more time."

I will die never knowing what propelled him through this life. Later, when I met him as a worldly adult, I understood he was a man of obligations that protected him from the things he was afraid of and from the things he did not truly want. But I never understood the difference. Perhaps he didn't either.

* * *

Mercy has returned from her morning swim. Her cheeks are flushed with the speckled glow of healthy sun. Her skin is a little too fair for unrelenting exposure, and her freckles are more prominent than usual. She wears sunblock as she should, or at least enough to avoid confrontation with her mother, who, when she is not overseeing my meals, guards her offspring like a canine spirit. *Give us both some more space,* I think. Mercy, awaiting more news of Josip, has parked herself comfortably on the edge of the bed, her head propped on her hand as she leans on her elbow. I move my dinosaurian legs to make room. She knows I am her toy. I put down my Turgenev, marking my place carefully, although I have read this one dozens of times before.

"Soon we girls were transported away to work for the Germans. When I learned later what they had done to the Jews, I thought he had perished." I say this matter-of-factly. I do not wish to recount the history of war in Ukraine.

"Babushka, did you see him again?"

"I saw him again here in America. Years later." This confuses her, and she reaches for her carrot juice. It reminds me of the cake they don't let me have either. She notices the knotted blue and red tributaries of blood strangling my sorry stumps of legs.

"I knew Josip when I was a very young girl, and I met him again when I was much older. It was more than twenty-five years between sightings." I laugh. "When I saw him again, quite by accident, on a street in Manhattan, he told me he had had a number tattooed on his forearm. He had managed to burn it off somehow. It had left an unsightly scar that filled me, when I looked on it, with a sadness of the world as I had not known before. That Josip was something else."

Mercy remains still and wide-eyed. I have not received this kind of attention since Lavrentii was a toddler. I can see that much is not clear to the mind of this gentle child of privilege and affluence.

"Babushka, I'm confused. I thought Joseph wrote you letters."

"Oh yes, my dear, but that was much later. My first encounter was so long ago and very far away. When his hair was silky dark and his skin was as smooth as a peach, like yours, he gave me the pomegranate. We were children. I wasn't much older than you are now. Josip the elder is a story for another day. I'm tired now, my little pigeon."

I close my eyes. I want to remember this inauspicious tryst—the day, the lunch, the man, his smoke, his fingers, his eyes, the shaved dark stubble of his weathered cheek. The memory is as vivid as this morning's breakfast and as thick, heavy, and sweet in my mind as a large dollop of maple syrup. I would have smeared Josip's scar with cinnamon and sugar and licked it from his arm right there on Forty-Second Street, but we were dignified, well-dressed cosmopolites in an easily outraged public place.

"Babushka, will you tell me about Josip tomorrow?"

"We will see my, darling. I must rest now. The needle makes me so tired."

Josip

I am walking alone along Seventh Avenue away from the theater, where I have just bought two tickets for an evening's performance of—I do not remember the play, because I am so distracted later. It is likely some desiccated Russian émigré production full of nostalgia and boring ennui, a request from Lavrentii Sr., whose orphaned sensibility has never succeeded in cutting ties to the motherland. But today, right now, I can see the image, in my mind's eye, of this familiar stranger, his brown tweed jacket covered by a black coat with the fur collar, his black leather gloves distressed by wear. As I walk, I look down, repulsed by the sight of a corpulent roach the size and shape of a beech leaf moving sluggishly along the sidewalk. It must be garbage day in the city. I do not notice the man in front of me until we collide. With that look of revulsion and irritation, I look up to see an older Josip standing in front of me. I am struck dumb by the sight of this apparition. His bituminous curls have taken on an even distribution of grays. He recognizes me immediately. "Eva," he says in the Russian way. *Yeva.* He remembers my name. I don't recall the first words we exchange, for I have been struck by lightning—again. How do we manage to make our way to the deli? It is one of those famous ones in New York, with pictures of grinning luminaries all around. We sit at the bar. I notice he is wearing a thick wedding band of gold and black in patterns reminiscent of Spanish Toledo. We order sandwiches, and while we wait, he lights a cigarette, an unfiltered Camel. He inhales deeply, and when he releases, I try to catch his smoky exhaust. His face is the dark leather of a man who has spent too much time in the sun. Around his chin has gathered a heaviness that announces prosperity and a kind of power that comes with having to make small decisions regularly. But his eyes are as soft as those of the young boy he used to be. He seems genuinely happy to see me, though he is slightly agitated. He fidgets by flicking his thumb on the cigarette while he smokes.

He tells me about his family. He has a wife in Israel.

"We live in Haifa," he says through the smoke as he pulls pictures from an inside pocket. His son will soon be conscripted into the army. He worries. His daughter is studying medicine. "Her name is Eva," he announces, as if there is no particular significance to be assigned to this singular fact. A coincidence? He is proud of her. His demeanor is somewhat formal, and he speaks as if we are acquaintances with no specially shared memories. "I met my wife in the camps. We survived because we were stronger. Maybe we were just lucky." He shows me the burn scar on his arm but does not mention his mother or father. I am afraid to ask. He squints and looks directly into my eyes as if he is waiting for something or reading my mind. I tell him about Tailfingen and the Allied bombs, how we ran from them in terror while hoping they would reach their intended targets; about Panas and Lavrentii, husbands number one and two; and about Lavrentii Jr., who is eleven at that time. But I say nothing about the blue-eyed German soldier who took me off to the hollow, the sounds I heard when I ran, my brother who died, or my father, whose history remains perpetually in darkness. Betrayal is not a subject for casual conversation.

He continues to smoke while looking at me in a way I do not understand, which brings on an inner rapture that I am loathe to reveal. In those moments, I am a woman of the world. I sparkle even as my hand trembles. Surely my heart races. I desire to take his smoking cigarette and put its wetness to my lips, to take away from this meeting as much as I can of this man's physical presence.

We agree to meet when he is in the city for business. I would like to throw my arms around him like a child—like the child I was the last night he came to my window—but I am afraid he will be dismayed by my effusiveness. I know it will not please him somehow. "Do you remember when we last met?" I ask, and I immediately regret what I perceive to be a parochial question. He merely nods and looks down at his shoes.

In this small gesture, I sense a fine sliver of hope. I have dreamed poems around this man and cannot believe the sudden good fortune to have a second chance, no matter how diminished in possibility. We exchange addresses and make plans to meet again. As we prepare to take leave of one another, Josip suddenly takes my hand and kisses it in the European way. In my mind, his lips seem to linger for a split second too long.

I never mention the meeting to Lavrentii Sr.

Lavinia

Yesterday was uneventful. We had fish and vegetables, some sort of greens—nutritious, of course—for dinner. It was all tasty but without sweetness. We made pleasant banter about the state of my health, my high spirits, and everyone's good works. If they took dessert, they did it, thankfully, out of my sight. Lavrentii and Lavinia had worked together preparing the meal. Later, while Mercy swam with Maribel and her mother performed lifeguard duty, Lavrentii and Lavinia audibly engaged in happy lovemaking. I read my faithful Turgenev, every so often looking up to watch the swimmers from my screened-in porch. Even the sweet whisperings from the concupiscent couple next door could not derail my concentration. Turgenev, for me, feels like an exercise in recall—a recurring dream in which there are no longer variations, a faithful old friend to whom

I have become accustomed, a kind of security blanket. I have read this edition of *Fathers and Sons* so often that I swear I could rewrite it from scratch. I want to be buried with Bazarov's story—but not because it reminds me of my own. Bazarov and I are different. I would never die for love.

* * *

"Lance, you have to talk to her, because if you don't, I shall."

It appears that yesterday's mood of bonhomie has dissipated. I am being reprimanded for "stealing"—her word—chocolate pudding. Because I spooned a tiny bit from Mercy's dish into my mouth? She speaks in front of me as if I'm not in the same room, as if I have been declared incompetent. *Not so fast, dear daughter-in-law.* What will happen to my Lavrentii when I am gone? He'll have to live with that effete Lance name with which she has dubbed him, as if he were a performing extra, a character on the set of *The Great Gatsby*. He went to Princeton as a diffident Lavrentii, a modest Larry, and returned a prancing Lance, a veritable southern gentleman, with a potent matricide on his arm, Lavinia—otherwise known as Electra, by my sights. Would her scientific mind make the connection?

"Mother, we have been making all kinds of sacrifices for you. It hurts me that you do not accept the gravity of your condition. We have come here for your sake."

My sake? The very nerve. I recall the times I waited hand and foot on them when I was healthier. They'd say, "Ask Babushka to watch Mercy tonight. She doesn't mind." Yes, it was a pleasure, to be sure, but sometimes an imposition. I never refused them. Lavrentii is too much like his father—a milksop. *Stand up to her! Why don't you?* He thinks I don't understand that she wanted some distraction for her daughter. I think she has abandoned any hope that I will teach Mercy a couple of words of Russian, although I manage to punctuate my thoughts with expressions or words from the past. Russian, Ukrainian—it's all the same to me now. Does Lavinia realize there's a difference between the two languages? By this time, she must know that Ukrainian is a real language with its own syntax and cultural heroes, not some substandard argot spoken by ignorant peasant trash. Taras Shevchenko? The story "Taras Bulba"? The Yul Brynner movie is before her time. Gogol was Ukrainian—a madman, though. Bulgakov was born in Kiev. *What can she know? Ignorant interloper. Arriviste.* My anger makes me say these words under my breath.

"I beg your pardon, Mother?"

"I was thinking of *gogul mogul.* My mother used to prepare it for me when I was a child. I don't know why it suddenly came to me." I smile and look wistfully away as if I am remembering a golden moment from my childhood. "Egg yolk with sugar. It was dreadful."

She looks at Mercy, exasperated. My lovely child does not look up; she does not give her mother the satisfaction. "Mercy, are you meeting Maribel later?" Lavinia asks.

I learn that Maribel's mother is driving the girls to the Glass Museum in Sandwich. Why doesn't Lavinia just let the girl play? She's always organizing Mercy's time so that she doesn't have to waste her own. *A soldier for education. Marsch!*

"I would gladly have stayed at home with Branka. She has been helping me for years now. Ever since Lavrentii Senior died. You see, I have managed to stay alive despite the absence of your goodwill and careful ministrations." I am high-minded and saccharine. You can catch more flies with honey.

"Branka is not a doctor. Your blood sugar is dangerously high. We're trying to stabilize it with diet and with medicine. If we cannot bring it down, your life will be hell."

She means *our* lives will be hell. Life is always hell. If it isn't this hell, it is another kind of hell. Hell is the baggage we carry. Old age and infirmity teach us that happiness is sweet because it is impermanent. In the language of the new age, old age sucks. What would she do if I said that to her face? She wouldn't let Mercy near me. She would send her off to another continent. *Careful.*

I feign obedience. I am now the compliant, accommodating old lady. "Lavrentii, it's time for my shot." The tone of my voice is frail and beseeching. He softens. Electra rolls her eyes again but thinks I haven't noticed. When I'm gone, she'll take command. Poor Lavrentii with a golden heart. Surrounded by Amazons young, middle-aged, and old, he thinks the pursuit of spiritual understanding and the life of the mind will protect him.

Eva

It is interesting to see how far people will venture to the edge. Some will not go far. They hug what is known—the tree, the rock, the door. Some go to the edge, look over it often, revel for a short time in the exhilarating sense of danger, and then retreat. The last group is like the second, but each encounter with the edge brings them closer to the terror and magnificence of flight. When that moment arrives, they topple over; some continue toppling headlong into the ravine, while others recover and soar into wind, where they gain power and perspective. Each group is different but interesting for the same reason. Why members in each group behave as they do is the reason stories are told and novels are written.

My first husband, Panas, was a member of the second group. He was an intellectual who, despite his dalliance with peril, remained close to what is known. He told me he had seen Lenin rail against the czar and the middle classes in St. Petersburg before it became Leningrad. Now it's St. Petersburg again. You would think that tyrants could learn from history. Panas was considerably older than me and better educated. He knew languages and history. We émigrés had learned German and lived history, and some of us were lucky enough to survive it. I admit to seeking only my own happiness. What had I seen until then? I saw famine, destruction, and disappearance. I saw people separated from family and torn from their homes. Il'ko died. My father wrote to me to tell me the news. He wrote in an even, unhurried hand, as if all life had been squeezed from his fingers. His curled underlines and ornate Gothic-like capitals were deflated like broken balloons. His embellished style was flattened by his profound sorrow. I didn't recognize the script when the letter came. Mother had barely a third-grade education, so Papa had to write: "Il'ko was killed." I learned later the circumstances of his death. They found him with a German bullet to his head, execution style. By the time the letter reached me, I was married to Lavrentii's father. I can see the word *ubit* written in purple ink—so long ago now—on Russian stationery, which used to have the feel of thick newspaper ready to yellow and disintegrate in time for the next issue. How he must have struggled to attach the name of an only son to that ghastly word: *killed*. His handwriting used to dance across the line with dramatic flourish. He was prouder of his penmanship than he was of his children. It seemed like an anomaly—a semibrute of a man with great penmanship. What did that say about him? He possessed vanity, affectation, an inner life, a personality refusing the constraints of location? Imagine this same semibrute devoid of all exception, a perfect null—transparent, invisible but for grief. He taught me that we are unique, as should be our handwriting. I think he expected me to come home. But by that time, Panas had died, and Lavrentii Sr. and I along with the other displaced persons were running from the Soviets. We were waiting for papers. We thought America was the remedy for all of our ills. It was the land of big cars, of laughter and forgetting. What kind of life could I have after what I had done? How could I turn my back on a future that, for the first time in my short life, promised freedom from grief and maybe even personal amnesty?

I was confused, though, by a question that has followed me from one country to another, from one kind of life to another as far from the first as the constellations in the sky. It is a question that cannot be squelched or strangled, a question about duplicity that has stalked me by night and by day; surprised me in the middle of mundane tasks, such as chopping vegetables, stirring soup, or frying onions;

pulled me by force from the most harmless of places; and propelled me to the brink of hell. It is a question that will forever prevent my return to a family—or what remains of it—I had left as a child. "I never understood, Papa, how the German with the blue eyes knew to come to the house of the man with exceptional penmanship. How did he know my name? Papa, how did he know I was the one to ask? Did you think that your only son would be spared? Didn't you understand you were placing your head into the mouth of a dragon?"

* * *

"How old were you then, Grandma?"

We have succeeded in navigating the treacherous waters of family lunch, and I am back in my room with my head propped against the pillows. I am resting. Mercy has been interrogating me on my brilliant life with the émigrés. Despite my desire to hear of her adventures on the beach with Maribel, we have nose-dived and crash-landed into the events of my first marriage. Her persistence is overpowering.

"By then, I was twenty." I draw the words out reluctantly but am eager to get past this short and unpleasant history. "Panas was nearly forty but looked older, at least to me. He didn't have much longer to live. Of course, I didn't know it then. If I had, I might have acted differently."

"What do you mean, Babushka?"

The unavoidable has arrived. When Mercy was a toddler, I used to hate that Lavrentii taught her to call me Babushka. It made me feel older than I wished, although I was old even then. Now it makes me feel old-world ancient and loved. I know that when Mercy uses the name, she is being especially tender. The word *babushka* is Slavic. It reminds me of Russian women festering with possibility, sitting on fences, looking upon fields of wheat, dreaming of lives outside of the narrow proscriptions of the village. This one word makes me think of the sweetness of children and the nearness of death. Suddenly, I feel hungry for an Oreo cookie.

"Babushka, did you hear me?"

I am startled out of my short reverie. "Sorry, my love. What?"

"How would you have acted differently?"

I am still confused.

"With Panas. You said if you had known he would die soon, you would have acted differently."

"I think I blamed myself. We always blame ourselves when we lose the ones we love. It's a kind of survivor's guilt. You've heard of that, haven't you?" I hesitate. I am not sure I should tell Mercy how I felt then, but I soldier on. "When he got sick, I couldn't bear to be near him. He stopped eating, grew cadaverous, and died. Toward the end, he stank—he couldn't help it, but he stank. I can never forgive myself for letting him see how his deterioration repulsed me."

"But, Grandmother, I thought you loved him?" Mercy is too young to understand how speech betrays her. She has dropped the *Babushka*. Using the word *Grandmother* is her way of disapproving.

"I loved him in a different way. Perhaps he was the gentle father I never had."

Mercy picks up the framed picture of Lavrentii Sr. and touches the glass gently, as if by so doing, she can commune with the grandfather she never knew.

"What a mustache on Grandpa. Did he have it when you met him?"

"*Okh, Tzvetochek*. It was a uniform, a kind of style that belonged to his class. He was educated and very learned at a time when there weren't so many intellectuals. Not like today. They're a dime a dozen. Everyone knows more than his neighbor—like most New Yorkers, who feel it is their responsibility to tell you all they know and demonstrate all the languages they speak as soon as they meet you."

"Don't you like people from New York, Babushka?"

"Only the ones that don't talk."

"Mama's from New York." She eyes me suspiciously.

"We lived in New York for a long time and met all sorts of people. I'm talking about a frame of mind—that's all." I evade the question. Mercy will not pursue it. She is too intelligent.

"Was he a teacher, Babushka? Grandpa, I mean." I was right.

"A teacher. A historian. You already know he dabbled in novels. Wrote under a pen name. Like Mark Twain."

"Wow, Grandma. Was he as famous as Mark Twain?"

"No, darling. He never became truly famous. But in the émigré community, he was known and largely respected, although I must tell you those émigrés were always squabbling amongst themselves and flaunting their superior blood, getting fat on pork while gossiping about each other."

"Didn't he gossip too?"

"Well, darling, for all of his flaws, he was a big man; he was gracious and generous. I met him in Germany. He had been Panas's student, and he helped me get over Panas's death. For all of their high-minded twaddle, the émigrés were full of poison. I think they blamed me for letting Panas die. How ridiculous." I marvel as I shake my head. "The cheek, the bloody cheek. *Proklyatie Duraki*. Damned fools. I'm guilty of many things, my dear, but not cancer." I am seized by a laughing fit. Mercy pats me gently on the back until it subsides, and she hands me a glass of water that is always there for such eventualities. I wipe away the tears that have been brought on by my theatrical outburst. "But for Grandfather Lavrentii, I would have been ostracized by the émigrés. He had a crush on me, I think, while he was my first husband's student. And at first, he was very shy." I am suddenly an old coquette again. Perhaps this is why those émigrés suspected me of ill. "I liked him too. He seemed so very educated and smart for one so young. Besides Russian, he knew German and French, and he was learning English. English, by the way, wasn't so important until after the war. People didn't learn it routinely the way they do today. When I asked him why he had insisted on learning the German language so well, he answered that German was the language not only of the Nazis but also of many illustrious Germans that had come before, like Goethe, Schiller, Schopenhauer, Hölderlin, and Von Kleist." She scrunches her nose at names she is unlikely to know. "These were big names for European intellectuals. I was so impressed by all of this and his modesty as well." Whether this statement is entirely so matters less than that she believes it to be. He certainly knew his strengths no matter his humility. "Shortly after the war ended, we were waiting for sponsors and approvals and papers to come to America. Munich—where I met him—was like a ghost city. You could hear your footsteps on the cobbled streets, and there was a palpable sense of death in the air. We were happy to be going to America, because there was so much that felt unclean in this old world."

"Palpable, Grandma?"

"You could touch it, taste it, as if you'd leaned over and put your hand in fresh pigeon droppings or a stranger's saliva."

"Ekhhh, Grandma, that's nasty." She laughs as she recoils at the thought.

* * *

In the morning, we awoke shivering. It had rained the night before, and the sun, beginning to warm the grasses as far as the eye could see, had cast a rainbow over the landscape. From the enclosure, we could see over the bushes to the road, where a muzhik had parked his horse. We watched him disappear into the trees, probably to relieve himself. The man's horse—or was it a donkey?—stood with an enormous erection, its member extended nearly to the ground like a proboscis divining for drink. High above its inscrutable equine head was one of nature's miracles: mist and prismatic sunlight forming bands of shimmering color, as if to fool us into believing in the world's inexhaustible beauty. As Josip lay there with a fine sheet of moisture on his body, I wiped a bit of spittle from the corner of his mouth and licked it from my finger. It tasted of sweetness and cinnamon, like the *rugallahs* from the night before. With his eyes closed, Josip didn't notice the tiny yellow spider scurrying across his forehead, perhaps in search of dry ground to begin spinning the work of the day. "Look, Josip," I whispered. "A rainbow, a gift from God."

* * *

"Someday you will meet the one, *Tzvetochek*—someone who will feel like the perfect complement to your piece of the puzzle, someone who will fit like a glove. And you both will know it. But you must have the courage to take it before it is lost again. Do not be afraid to love generously, my darling."

"Was that how it was with you and Josip?" Mercy's eyes brighten at a world of infinite possibilities. Someday she too will dream these things.

"You can love another in different ways. Sometimes you love because you admire, and you want what you admire. You even want to become what you admire. By loving in that way, you gain qualities.

"Sometimes you love another because of the way that person makes you feel."

"Was that how you loved Josip, Babushka?"

"Well, partly. I loved your grandfather more for the way he made me feel—until, that is, he started hallucinating. The old codger."

Mercy giggles. She suddenly avoids my eyes. Does she remember his ill temper? I continue. "He used to make me feel beautiful and important. He was once young and handsome, you know. And when he complimented me on my figure and my hair, it made me feel jubilant. He didn't realize that not everybody saw the world through his eyes. That's why he started accusing me of all sorts of indiscretions." I draw the word *indiscretions* out for Mercy's sake. I want to see her eyes hunger.

"Like what, Grandma?"

"Of looking at other men." Her eyes tell me she wants to know more. "Of course I looked at other men, thought about them. I wasn't blind and never short on imagination. You always know when there is interest. It is like a scent to a bloodhound—the inclination of the body, the movement of the hands, the hovering." I drop my book and wave my hands like an Indian dancer. I'm always looking for a laugh.

"But I'm digressing again. We were talking about love, *nyet*?"

"Was that how you loved Josip?" She repeats the question even as she smiles at my hand acrobatics.

Again, I avoid the question directly. "Sometimes one loves because one has no choice—with a feeling as true as it is animal, a feeling as pure as one's love for one's grandchildren."

"You mean the way you love me?"

"In a way, yes. The way I love you. My desire for Josip was elemental, cellular."

"Babushka, what does *cellular* really mean?"

"Ask your mother, darling; she's the scientist."

Lavinia

"Cellular? What is all this 'cellular' nonsense? What on earth have you been feeding my Mercy?"

It is later in the afternoon. Mercy has gone on her rendezvous at the Glass Museum. Lavrentii has dragged a chair and a book out to the water, where he can avoid the shimmering heat of the *resol*. He has placed the chair at the water line as the tide recedes. A while ago, I saw Lavinia disappear into the ocean for a long, expiatory swim. A kind of heavy tranquility of sound and ocean has settled over our cottage while I, in my rocker, drift, nodding into intermittent sleep between bouts with Bazarov. Suddenly, I am startled by a visitation from my savior, who has risen and returned from the waters: the grande dame of neuromedicine. As I open my eyes, Lavrentii is making his way back home.

Oh, so now it's "my Mercy." She has walked in barefoot with a plush red-and-yellow towel wrapped around her hips. Although she tries to hang back and appear casual and random, I sense from the way she stands—arms akimbo, legs at attention—and from the directness of her speech, which is without polite flourish, the pugnacious and confrontational nature of this visit. I suppose she doesn't need a babysitter at the moment. Lavinia's eyes have turned purple. Lavrentii has just come in. The tone of her voice is controlled, but make no mistake—she is charging like a wild Cossack falsely accused of cowardice. It is the ire of the outraged. I wonder if she is putting on a show for Lavrentii's benefit. "And what's all this about a donkey's organ and running away from home? Mother, what foolish ideas are you filling her head with?"

Go on—say it. Dick, dick, dick. Donkey's dick. "I was telling her about my childhood in the Ukraine." I answer her questions as honestly as I can. I cackle under my breath like the old harridan that I am, but outwardly, I remain dignified.

"Your childhood?" she repeats. She stares at Lavrentii, who has not spoken a word since coming in. He remains standing like a statue at the door. He hardly expected to be greeted this way. *Surprise!*

"Unedited." I look her hard in the eyes. I offer no contrition. Suddenly, I picture Lavinia baked with a honey-tarragon glaze and an apple in her mouth, her Graves' eyes ready to explode. "That was how I remembered it. Do you suggest I should have told her fairy tales?"

"But, Eva, this is a thirteen-year-old child. It is a dangerous and unpredictable world out there."

"Tell me something new, why don't you?" I say it quietly, but I am annoyed at this jarring intrusion on my inner life. My neck has seized up at the abruptness of the assault, and I am visibly in pain. As suddenly as it comes on, her demeanor softens. *Now it's "Ee-va" again, is it? Will she throw me into the street? Or do I detect an ever-so-slight turning back?* Lavinia is not nearly as high-minded as she is high-strung, but she suddenly understands she has transgressed an invisible line. Lavinia is a woman who spends her life studying her own behavior. Often, she acts first and regrets later. She has constructed herself from the shards of a broken home. She was discarded by a negligent and abusive parent. I don't know that for sure. She has never spoken to me about it, except generally. I have never met her mother, who is institutionalized, she says. Can you imagine? And the father is dead. Allegedly dead. She has given no more detail. I never probe. She never offers. I think she lives in shame, but I don't know why, and I am too old and tired to care. She has done well for herself with my Lavrentii, but she will always lack the grace her own daughter carries naturally. She resents Mercy for it. I know she is aware that I know so.

"Oh, come on now, Luv." It is Lavrentii, weighing in on his mother's side.

"No, you come on." She is still somewhat shrill but subsiding. There is an unstated wrong she wants to redress. I suspect it has nothing to do with Mercy—or with me, for that matter.

"I told her about my first love and about the war, about some of the things I saw. That's all. She is interested."

Lavinia sighs as she sinks deeply into the blue divan. Judiciously, she avoids my eyes, as if there is danger in an old lady's gentle reproach. I detect the beast deconstructing. She will not err so flagrantly next time. This was good practice in a controlled environment. I take advantage of the moment. This round goes to me.

"What's for dinner? Will we eat soon? Isn't it time for my shot?" *Careful, Eva,* I tell myself. One must be gracious in victory.

Mercy

I am watching. Lavinia has come to the breakfast table with swollen eyes, as if she has slept badly or has spent the night weeping. I suspect it is both. Lavrentii smiles at me as he pulls up a chair. There is such kindness in his look. I think this not because I am his mother but because he is his father's son. I have been exceptionally blessed. Mercy has just come in wearing the same blue bathing suit she wore yesterday. She plants an aromatic buss on my forehead. I try, unnoticed, to absorb her smell. *My peach, my apricot, my lovely purple plum.*

"Did you sleep well?" Lavrentii asks politely. How I dislike polite questions even after so many years, and the polite answers they encourage.

"I dreamed of your father."

"Grandma, will you tell me your dream?"

"Later, my pigeon. After breakfast, when we're alone." I roll my eyes and smile at my pristine grandchild, all in jest. I play the old coquette again. I mean no special collusion. It is our game and our time together, and no matter how I am feeling, the time with her is my treasure. She smiles. To think that this lovely creature enjoys my company. I am dumbfounded but, above all else, grateful for this.

"Why don't you tell us all, Eva?" Lavinia feigns a lightness of tone, but her words are heavy with challenge. On this morning, of all mornings, I wish no confrontation. I am old and have slept badly. I am tortured by pain churning endlessly in my legs and needles in my brain. I want to shout, "Do you have no shame?"

"You don't need to, if you would rather not," my son says.

Bless you, Lavrentii. "Do you mind peeling the kiwi for me?" I ask without a trace of irony.

"But I would like to hear it as well. Perhaps it needs to be censored," Lavinia says. On a thin dime, she has slipped dangerously, but she immediately regrets her words. She is still smarting from yesterday's defeat. I'm certain of it.

This calls for a little righteous indignation. "Perhaps I should allow you to install a listening device in my room in case I misbehave."

"Stop it. Both of you." Lavrentii is growing tired of all of this madness. All he wants is a little amity between his dying mother and clawing wife, a jot of tranquility for himself.

"I saw young Lavrentii Sr. calling to me from the opposite side of a ravine. He was holding a bouquet of spiked red dahlias in one hand and beckoning to me with the other. I saw myself running to the edge of a mountain and making myself ready for the plunge. But when I leaped, it was airy. I bounced back up several times. The sensation of flying through trees and waterfalls was exhilarating. Only once before in my life have I had such a dream." This is mostly true. Right before the knock on my window, I must have drifted into a field of sunny haystacks. It was on that night. It was so many years ago that it is a wonder I remember it. I did not sleep much while waiting for Josip to come, but when he did, it was as if we had been lifted away by a bouncing balloon carrying us from haystack to glistening haystack, though it was nighttime, and the only reflection from the ground must have been the light of the moon. Since then, my reveries have been populated by menacing yet oddly familiar creatures with daggers and guns in their eyes, resembling men only barely, approaching from both sides of a small bridge from which there is no exit.

"I wonder—are we capable of dreaming of faces we have never seen?" I pose this thought as a legitimate question but mainly as a deflection of the matter at hand. I look past Lavinia quickly to Mercy, but for a split second, our eyes meet.

"I don't think you can dream of people you have never seen," Mercy answers. Oh, how I adore her innocence. "But perhaps you can create composites in your mind, no? A nose from one attached to the mouth and teeth of another and held together by the eyes of someone else. And then they are unrecognizable. What do you think?" Mercy smiles and looks away, as if she is imagining.

"I'll tell you more later," I say to Mercy. "But anyway, that is the gist of my dream, really. I don't remember how it ended. Maybe I fell into the ravine." I cackle as Lavinia abruptly leaves the table.

She returns with a loaf of cinnamon toast with raisins and places it on the table.

"Do you intend to eat that in front of me?" I understand she wants war, but for the first time, I am not up to it. "What have I done, Lavinia? Do you believe I could harm Lavrentii's daughter? Don't you understand there is no one in the world dearer to me?" I sense a slight shudder of glee in my adversary. In a moment of exhaustion, I have revealed my Achilles' heel. Have I lost the war?

Lavinia has collected herself to prepare the offense. "Eva, I expected you would be a civilizing influence on my daughter." I catch the word *my*. "Instead, you are teaching her curse words and filling her head with X-rated foolishness about running away from home. Do you understand what it is to be homeless?" She says this as she is buttering her cinnamon toast.

"As a matter of fact, I do."

My eyes widen at the memory of the flavor of the rugallahs. I feel the saliva collecting at the back of my mouth. *Save me, someone. Save me, please.*

"Mom, can Grandma have a piece of raisin toast?" Mercy asks.

My darling, my darling, my darling child.

"Of course not, Mercy. You know what this will do to her blood sugar."

"But then why do you eat it in front of her? Papa and you have always said you shouldn't eat the things you cannot offer in front of others. Why do you suddenly break the rules with Grandma?"

Lavrentii suddenly rises from the table like a mountain from the sea. The chair vibrates against the ceramic floor as he lifts to action. Without a word and without expression, he picks up the loaf and, as two slices fall to the floor, tosses it into the trash. He picks up the errant fresh slices and relegates them to the same mangled fate. He turns to me silently, and as he is about to take my arm to lead me back to my room, Lavinia begins weeping, gasping with deep, inconsolable breaths. Mercy stands, stunned.

Poor, damaged doctor of neurophysiology, I think. I am certain I shall not be here to see how this story ends. But somewhere inside, I am profoundly sorry for it all.

Lavinia Speaks

I

I am confounded by Eva. I am not the enemy.

She seemed to come unhinged after Mercy was born—not totally but enough to be noticeable, at least by me, by my standards. But not immediately. It is strange how a single incident can change the connection between two people. It was the butter. I remember it. She kept slathering butter on bread and giving it to a three-year-old Mercy, who gobbled it up as if it were ice cream. Lance and I had just come back from dinner with a couple of my colleagues. We had left Mercy with Eva, who I thought would give international context to my child. "International context" was Lance's sneering remark. Why not expose children to whatever cultural influences can give them a head start in this world? This isn't crass ambition, just family politics. Anybody would, under the circumstances, do the same for his or her child. However, when we picked her up, there she was, eating bread and butter and laughing with her grandmother. *Kleb s maslom*—that's the one phrase I have managed to learn in that utterly impenetrable language. But there was Mercy, sputtering away while stuffing her little mouth with bread and butter. "How much butter have you given her?" I asked in a measured tone, although I wanted to make clear I did not approve of the child's ingestion of so much fat. There was no reproach whatsoever in my voice.

Eva barely looked up at me. She kissed Mercy good night and left for bed, claiming a headache or something like that. Lance told me on the way home I shouldn't have spoken to her so harshly. I didn't give it much thought, and I didn't apologize. I wanted it to be clear as daylight that Mercy should eat a balanced diet. And it didn't happen again. Eva seemed to have forgotten the incident. She was, after all, always happy to see Mercy. She would scoop her up into her arms and secret her away for their time together.

II

When she lay on the sidewalk, it was friggin' me who had to pick her up and cajole her back to the house. I hated going out at that hour; I was terrified someone from the school would spot me. It happened night after night, drink after drink. While in her stupor, she would stroke my cheek, call me her baby, and tell me how much she loved me, her darling, darling pumpkin. She called me her pumpkin because I was round. I ate potato chips, cookies, and Mounds bars while watching out for her and keeping on top of my schoolwork. They kept me awake and on the ready for eventualities. My skin was spotted and rough; I had no time for vanities or creams, just work. The high school's most-popular guy called me Spotty once. It cut me to the quick. Now he's working at a plumbing job; he has lots of money but no cachet.

Charlie Lewis, my physics teacher, came looking for her to tell her I had great potential, but she slept through it all. He understood. He called me out for academic recognition, nominated me for scholarship, and he helped me through those times. But I dreamed of him in a checkered shirt with a leer in his look after he took me for a steak dinner, ostensibly to discuss my future. I had potential, he told me again and again. I could be illustrious. It didn't matter. I was seduced by the illustrious. Why not after you've cleaned your mother's vomit and piss and unmentionably more from the kitchen's broken linoleum? After you've scraped it from the cracks so that the smell wouldn't linger? Charlie, as the kids called him, helped me, and the moneymen took pity on me. They saw worth and possibility—"strength in the face of domestic adversity" was the way they put it. Those fancy schools were looking to go low brow, wanting to diffuse that sacred blue blood with a bit of authenticity, with fiery red, to break up the genes that were devouring themselves in orgies of deluded self-adoration. They listened to Charlie because he was one of them, although it didn't help him with his kids when he was jumping from chemistry lab counters to demonstrate the laws of science. He was a loser, an intellectual, and my sponsor before the men and women who mattered. The blue-blooded fabulists hadn't the backbone to run the world, to confront its anomalies. They needed help from the earthy laborers who could sometimes match brain for brain and overwhelm by strength. Physical, moral, ethical—that was me. I read books easily—science books. I learned the world from the cellar, not through the thick lens of theory. Words always seemed vacant without the concrete to prop them up and to solder them to their theoretical constructions. So the men and women with money took me in and lavished me with praise. They backed their accolades with stipend after stipend year after year because I delivered and didn't disappoint, knowing this was my only ticket out of my mother's legacy of self-annihilation. I got fancy then, too. I stopped eating chips. My weight fell off; my skin peeled with lavish emollients and exfoliating agents; my hair, with daily washings and secret lightening agents, began to resemble corn silk; and my hands softened with moisturizing creams. Men began looking at me for me, no longer because of the compelling curiosity around my unorthodox provenance—that I had crawled high out of a ditch—although that remained, for many, a compelling reason to approach me. However, my eyes, lashes, hair, and succulent mouth became a more-compelling reason to stay, talk, examine, and hope. I knew I did not disappoint, and it made me more comfortable. It is a different feeling, allowing my smiles to flow naturally instead of ritualistically and giving warmth instead of searching for it from curious strangers and munificent benefactors.

I processed information quickly. My youthful unsightliness taught me to focus, to concentrate for relief on the concrete material world—inside my science and outside of budding desire and adolescent dismissal. I was a geek and a nerd and sexless behind the pounds and the zits. Besides, I could let no one discover the secrets of my domesticity, of maternal neglect and paternal malfeasance. I was proud and fragile. I felt it was better to face ignorance and neglect than disgust or pity from my peers. Charlie knew they were not my equals. Kind hearts, just as strength, can grow with adversity and failure, and adolescents must survive at all costs, often by destroying what they do not fathom. Mother Nature is wise in her cruelty, consequent in her pursuit of survival. I certainly owe mine to her.

But my mother had no cruelty in her, nor reserves. She gave me few weapons, but she taught me much—if not by design, then by default. She was guileless, so she was crushed beyond recognition when the man she called my father abandoned her in a hurry. If he was my real father, he gave no sign while he was around. If there was a biological link, he never let himself be swayed. If there was love, he ignored it. I cannot remember his face, but I can remember his freedom of body. He marched around the house buck naked, as if I were the proverbial potted plant, touching my mother in ways inappropriate for the eyes of a child. I remember how she chastised him, laughing at the pleasure that he doled out by measure. I said she had no reserve, and any rebuff by her was a fake show of remonstrance. She loved its cruelty, its humiliation. I hated the noise; the picture behind the noise; the groans; the naked, hairy ass of him; and the irrepressible brown dong. Each time, I ran to the farthest corner of the house, clenched my teeth, and squeezed my ears so tightly that I thought the lid on my scull would eject from its moorings. I opened my books, wherein everything had an order, fit by design, and where there was no order, I found it. Logic became my ally.

I was not yet twelve when he absconded. Once in a while, I get a Christmas card: "Deepest regards, Dad." But there is no return address, no picture—no anything. In the past, when I moved from dorm to dorm, the cards followed me around, and due to the perseverance of USPS, he managed to locate me. Even today he finds me, especially now that I am on the hospital roster with particulars accessible to anyone with a computer and inquisitive fingers. Even today I get the cards and look at them with a combination of confusion and dismissal before I pitch them summarily. I am not in the habit of pursuing ghosts. My X-rated memories of him pursue me with disgust even as I have forgotten his face.

III

I am confounded by Eva. I thought of us as friends or at least allies.

She loved food and company. The table always seemed to groan under the weight of all of her preparations. Although she herself never consumed excessively, she was always happy to see others stuffing themselves. These Slavs and friends of Slavs seemed to gather for hours around infinite dishes of multicolored foods, eating and smoking intermittently and drinking in small yet powerful increments while arguing most often about the state of the world and Russia's place in it, giving an old-world atmosphere to these boisterous and never-ending gatherings. It was as if the Second World War had never ended, and all of the other wars in between then and now were of little consequence. It was different from anything I had experienced. How curious that Lavrentii Sr. could act the firebrand in a crowd, while his diffident Eva maintained a reserved and steady presence. One could never be sure what she was thinking. How meek he would become as soon as all of the guests had left. There was a time when all of this seemed like magic to me, a romantic postwar movie in which my own true love was bringing me home. I was caught in a time warp that seemed fabulously cinematic and unreal.

It gave me a certain lifting cachet to talk about those dinners with my students and colleagues, who were amused. One of my lab mates used to salivate while I described, in delectable detail, the various menu offerings. *Zakuski*, Eva called them. Herring in cream sauce, stuffed grape leaves, meatballs swimming in forests of parsley and scallions, smoked sable—the list goes on and on. There was plenty of food to accompany all of the liquor they were swilling, mostly vodka. In those days, Lance could smile more often about his family's eccentricities. What he had taken for granted growing up and was even perhaps a bit shy about was a subject of grand curiosity for the rest of us born and bred in an America of fast-food hamburgers and cheese macaroni, and we were always hungry for new and unusual palatal adventures that did not involve Doritos or barbecue chips. "Why aren't you more like them?" I used to tease him.

"I am more like them than you understand," he would say, although he seemed, in style as well as in substance, to be fleeing from their influence. In fact, he did not smoke or drink, and when I met him, he was a vegetarian.

"You need protein," I would say, chiding him. "A little alcohol is good for the heart."

"But not good for the head" was the retort of the thin and intensely cerebral boy I could not have adored any more than I did.

IV

Lance was the first—and last—in a string of admirers to whom I could unburden myself. Like Shakespearean mercy, he drifted gently out of the sky to become a friend to me. He listened with kindness and gave insight to my thoughts, vent to my anger, and relief to my until-then-unnamed and unseen sorrow. He was shy where others were confident, was diffident where others asserted, and glowed softly where others shined glaringly. I saw him not only as lovely, for he was mightily handsome in a severe European way, but also as needing protection from the world and from his own innocence. His hair was nearly black, and his skin was white. His small eyes were closer than most, and his long, sharp nose unbalanced his face to the point where some saw him as exotic, others as handsome, and others not at all. He confided to me he hated his moniker. Lavrentii was no name for an American boy, and the name Larry was too churlish for his taste. Had he been a snob, would he have settled on me? I don't think so. He named himself Lance in the way of students away from home reinventing themselves when they no longer need to answer to overbearing mothers and demanding fathers. For him, coming from proud and educated immigrants who were not cowed by all-American attitudes, this was harder to do than for most.

Eva and Lavrentii Sr. welcomed me graciously into their home. They knew something of my history, but they did not seem to judge, nor did they probe for information. For this, I was grateful. But Eva continues to confound me.

I must confess I did want Eva to like me. I tried hard because she accepted me without examination. She must have sensed I would be mortified to narrate the details of my upbringing. We traveled together. In fact, when the old man was alive and I had just learned that I was pregnant with Mercy, we had a fabulous time in Venice. Eva had inexhaustible energy while wandering the streets and galleries, and for an old lady, she was adept with her new digital camera. Even then, she was odd. There were moments when she would stand at the edge of pavement or on canal bridges, staring long and hard into the sludgy waters. In one of those moments, when we had left the men to sit and discuss the receding foundation of the city, I offered a penny for her thoughts. "Your pennies are worthless here," she told me, looking me straight in the eye. It felt like a reprimand. Though the rest of our trip was wonderful, I remember that moment, which, at the time, seemed to cut me to the quick. Maybe it was the abrupt way she could cast off one face for another without skipping a beat or transform from Mother Teresa to Dracula without a word or incident of forewarning.

Otherwise, the early days were good. We all cooked and lunched as a team and giggled about love, men, and marriage. She seemed to fear nothing, and I wanted her to believe that I didn't either. Perhaps I tried too hard to demonstrate I was worthy of her son, of membership in her eccentric family. When I asked her direct questions about her life in Russia, she managed to utter some inanity before abruptly changing the subject, all while maintaining a smile. Lance warned me there were deep fissures of history she could not disclose and did not dare to reveal. When I asked him how he knew, he said he just did. So I felt Eva and I had much in common.

V

I am confounded by Eva.

Food has become an unbridgeable wedge between us.

It was my idea to come here. Mine! Knowing how much Eva loved Mercy, Lance thought she would agree, but he had his reservations. "What makes you think she will be grateful?" he said, twisting toward the door, as if escape would make the subject vanish.

"Gratitude has nothing to do with it," I countered. It would give us time to be together and to keep watch over his mother's diet, for she has an unconscionable habit of doing whatever she wants despite her infirmity. She is willful and unappreciative, as if she thinks the world owes her a deference package. Lance, my humanitarian, says her behavior is not due to a sense of entitlement; he insists she chafes at restrictions of any kind. It is not that she lacks discipline, according to him; it is that she has weighed her options and decided she will do only what is important for her emotional well-being. She knows she must die, but she intends to do it on her terms, not by begging favors from humans who cannot change the trajectory of her life except by an insignificant fraction. He knows his mother best of all. He believed she would come only because of Mercy.

* * *

Lance wonders out loud what I expected from this ocean idyll. He claims to have warned me about his mother's stubbornness. He thinks I wanted to will her into submission, as if she were a toothless dog—to make her thankful for her good fortune, her granddaughter, and her family. *Yeah, sure.*

On the other hand, I've done so much for her. I've gotten appointments with specialists it would otherwise have taken months to procure. And what does she do? The world is knocking at my colleague's door. Dr. J. J. Lothrop is a luminary in the field of internal medicine and a specialist on all forms of diabetes, and she treats him like a family retainer. "I don't want to do that," she tells him when he lists the foods she should avoid. "I don't care what happens to me," she says with a laugh when he tells her that without the daily shot, she will deteriorate rapidly. "I'm a mere shadow," she says when he tries to cajole her with compliments and praises her accomplishments, her learning, and her illustrious family. "Ha" is all she answers.

"Mother, please," I beg her in front of my indulgent and understanding colleague.

"Don't call me that," she protests. "My name is Eva."

How should I suffer her insolence and come away without contempt? I am mortified by Eva's behavior.

"Why do you professionals think you can define my future as if it were an equation on a piece of paper?" she asks me in the car while we're driving home. "Why do you discuss me while I am sitting in front of you, as if I am a laboratory animal?" she says with a laugh. "You medical professionals." She sighs and then looks away through the window. "Fancy office, nice view," she mutters.

Nonetheless, we undertake Dr. Lothrop's advisements. We—notice I said "we"—are to avoid highly glycemic foods, such as white rice and white bread. We are to encourage legumes and vegetables. We can have small amounts of bread but only if it's made with complex whole grains. Sweet jams and jellies are verboten. Some fruits, such as kiwi, have some vital element I can't remember. Oranges do too, but we cannot have too many, because they are high in sugar. Some melons are acceptable—never white melon, but watermelon, Eva's favorite, is okay in small amounts. I have been anointed caretaker. I hope Eva can live with this, as it will be temporary. She should be indebted to me, grateful that she has access to such privileged care. She came from nothing and nowhere and resents anyone for trying to bring comfort, if not to save her life. Lance tells me to leave it alone. I cannot, neither as a daughter nor as a physician. "I don't understand you, Lance! You are her son," I say.

"You're not really her daughter," he whispers, though I hear him. *He should be more concerned,* I think.

He tells me again she cannot be marginalized or shoved to the side in the matter of her own health or her own dying. "Leave her be," he warns. "She knows what she is doing."

He told me that before he turned eight or nine, she used to pray in church every Sunday, rain or shine. She seemed to have her own private dialogue with God and told no one what she prayed for. Lance said—how did he put it?—that her private susurrations preceded her as she glided, smooth and shoeless on waxed floors and Asian carpets, like an evening breeze through the hollowed chambers of their ample house. Lance used to describe her as though she were character in a Russian novel. He still does. Lavrentii Sr. used to make gentle fun, telling her that her actions, steeped in mumbo jumbo and superstition, were relics of a peasant upbringing. She ignored him. Lance often trotted along to the onion-domed basilica and was content to be able to sit and read his book when he was bored or to observe as he grew curious. The smells were magic to him, and he eventually, as an adult, came to understand how people could be stirred into the cauldron of belief through their senses and imaginations. He too came to believe that it was merely mumbo jumbo with stirring music impersonating revelation. At least that is what he says. But he also loved the postservice refreshments served by the old ladies. He got his Sunday fill of cabbage pierogi, he says, which was heaven. Who could think that something as prosaic as cabbage could fill a pastry worthy of the best eating establishments? The herring swimming in cream and apples was his favorite, but he would become so full of salt that Sunday afternoons at home were a lethargy of dreaming and sleep. He used to fill up his plate with pierogi and herring and take his prandial snack to a corner while his mother and Branka exchanged visits over coffee and pierogi of their own. I think he misses the food the most.

Then, one day, she stopped genuflecting, praying, and going to church. When he asked to be taken, she refused at first. She said she wanted nothing more to do with "those supplicating Orthodox zombies." Later she told him she would drive him there if he wished, but Lavrentii Sr., with residual political instinct still intact, nixed that. So it ended: the church, the supplication, the humility, and, for Lance, the Sunday morning pierogi and herring.

I am confounded by Eva. Her only friend seems to be Branka, one of those sweet, supplicating zombies she came later to summarily dismiss. She is no relation; she is a poor peasant woman who always kept plastic slip covers on her divan. I know this because of Lance's description of numerous postchurch visits. I must say this for Eva: she always treated Branka kindly, like an equal. This giant pillow of a woman has helped with the cleaning and cooking. Maybe Eva's friendship with Branca is her way of holding on to her own story. Lance tells me they are from the same village in the city of Mirgorod, which distinguishes itself famously as the birthplace of a mad Russian writer. When I humorously suggested that madness genes might be endemic to the village inhabitants, he pretended not to hear me. I can't imagine what Eva and Branka have talked about—the war, the escapes, the murders, Stalin?

When I defended the man of steel for hauling the Slavs into the twentieth century and introducing them to modernity, Lance looked at me as if I had lost my marbles. "It's never been just about washing machines and refrigerators," he muttered. "This is how you pretend to balance disgrace upon progress." These are his parting thoughts on the subject. I'm not sure what he means, but I understand when I need to stifle myself. That's what my father used to bark when my mother couldn't shut up: "Stifle." It is a wonder how much of my upbringing I owe to Archie Bunker. Those were the days.

It is a wonder that Lance and I, who come from opposite ends of the universe, have managed to make a baby.

Otherwise, Eva lives solitarily in a universe populated by ghosts. She seems lately to be losing her mind. This is not, strictly speaking, a medical diagnosis. On several occasions, as I have walked by her room, I have overheard her muttering to herself in any number of languages, as if she's speaking in tongues. When I walk in on one of her private reveries or call out "Mother!" the old lady just keeps muttering as if I am not there. I know she is pretending not to see me. When I nudge her softly, she becomes irritated and tells me to leave her alone. Yet Mercy can light up her face on a dime. Instantly aware of her presence, Eva greets her with kisses and hugs as though she had gone missing and is newly found. Each time Mercy comes in, it is the same thing: suddenly, Eva is normal again—whatever that means.

Lance loves her the way that sons love their mothers—defensively—and will have no discussion of this. "She has always talked to herself," he tells me. "Nothing has changed," he insists, "or perhaps it's changed only to a degree."

When I wonder out loud whether this is a further deterioration of her mind, he pounces on my use of "further deterioration." He says, "What gives you the idea that she is crazier than the rest of us? Who are you to make that determination? Leave her alone. She's content to wander where she is." He leaves me stunned and stupefied. I am not the villain here!

I'm certain she has not forgiven me for dragging her to the specialist. Instead of receiving thanks, I have become the pariah in this strange family.

VI

Yesterday Lance tossed the bread into the trash—the entire loaf. He flipped the lid of the can and sent it flying like a plump projectile, still encased in its crinkly cellophane wrapper.

Even Mercy deserted me.

Why shouldn't I be able to eat a piece of toast when I want to? When that pig of a father waltzed with his bare ass and limp dick past me through the kitchen, it broke my concentration. Sweet toast with butter or a cinnamon roll seemed to calm me until the next unwelcome incursion. Once, late at night, as I was studying for an honors class, he came out of the bedroom. The buzz from the fluorescent lamp in our kitchen added uncommon insult to the injury of bare yellow walls. While reaching for the Camels he had carelessly left on the table, he stood naked right next to me as I tried to learn the rules of binomial algebra. Even today, I can conjure up the smell of him, a mixture of residual tobacco smoke, male sweat, and female sexual discharge. He must have just done it with my mother and needed his smoke to ward off proverbial tristesse. "Whatcha studying?" he asked, drawing hard on his cigarette. When he bent to look at the fractions, the twisted hairs of his bare organ brushed acid against my arm.

Get out! Get away, you primate! You hairy beast! I thought. I wanted to scream, but "Math" was all I managed to sputter.

"You really understand that stuff, don't cha?" I shrugged, and he said, "Ya didn't get it from her." He blew O-shaped rings away from me in deference.

"How do you know who I got it from?" I asked him. "Just because she has her head in a bottle most of the time doesn't mean she was never up to the task of simple abstractions." Then I thought of her as the one who brought me to the window when I couldn't sleep, pointing to the stars and telling me the ones that shined the brightest were the residues of dead planets. She might have learned her constellations from the cheap horoscopes of the daily tabloids, but she knew them and managed to make them a source of wonder and comfort for a child afraid of the night. "There is more to her than meets the eye," I said, defending her to him.

"Yeah." He nodded, peering at me.

Does he know how disturbing his presence is? He smoked a while longer, pretending to study the fractions. It felt like hours, and then he was gone, along with his smile and his dark, hairy ass. But his smell lingered, and my concentration had been broken. I placed two pieces of cinnamon bread into the toaster and then opened the refrigerator and reached for the butter.

* * *

With no warning—at least to me—on a morning after a night before with my clueless mother, he was gone. Maybe he looked in on me before he left. I like to think I heard the door opening and felt his stale Camel aura hovering over my sleeping self. Maybe I dreamed it or hoped it. But why would I hope it, unless he meant something to me? He did not. But her pronouncement when she staggered out of the bedroom in the stupor that would from then on float silently around her head like cotton—that he was out of our lives—got mixed reviews from my subconscious. I suspected rightly that this would auger ill for our domestic situation, since he was paying the rent. In all fairness to him, he continued, however irregularly, to send money. It wasn't that I didn't trust him to deliver, however strange that might sound from someone who despised him; it was that my mother was incapable of taking control of practical necessities. Food, clothing, and shelter were beyond her ken, so they would fall to me, a fourteen-year-old chub of a girl with great aspirations, bursting pimples, and a less-than-steady hand on the pulse of the universe but a quick ability to learn the way things were done. If it hadn't been a twentieth-century melodrama, it would have looked like a Dickens tale. *Ludicrous.*

I don't know how we made it to my senior year. But by then, I had nailed it. With the help of Charlie Lewis, I was in—a poor, brainy duckling on her way to the Ivy League, having rightfully earned a chance to become a swan. Even the jocks started looking at me differently, although borrowing my assignments had been a regular occurrence during the college-prep years of school. My help had been insurance for me that they would protect me from insult and injury, and I could travel relatively unscathed through the cruel landscape of adolescence.

* * *

What was odd about my putative father is that he was comfortable with his body. He didn't seem to notice that his standing unencumbered might be discomfiting to a teenage girl, although he had done so for as long as I could remember. Lance, on the other hand, is private—not prudish or anything like that, just sensitive to the discomfiture of others. He would as soon commit hara-kiri on the palace steps as stand naked before his daughter. He understands the necessity of healthy distance—not just from his daughter but also from his mother, the neighbors, his colleagues at the institute, the world, and, regretfully, me. I have to laugh when he pulls the blinds before taking off his pants. He insists on the shades being drawn, the lights being out, and the level of noise being minimal when we are making love. He has always been kind and considerate to a fault, but he has never let me into the private world he inhabits. Whenever I have asked him what he is thinking, he changes the subject. But I know when he is annoyed with me. I understand the look: over his glasses and then quickly down with a tight mouth. There is silence where anger should be. At least with anger, one knows one's location in the scheme of an episode. It's how he looked today when he threw the bread into the trash. Privacy appears to be his refuge. I fear he is more like Eva than like his father. And Mercy is more like him than me. They have formed a cell to which I am, subliminally, seen as the invader. I am foreign among my own. This, I am afraid, bodes ill for the future of family harmony. Eva is the source, however innocent, of all of this unrest. I don't think Lance has ever told her about me, nor has she ever asked. Does she pretend, or is she not even remotely curious?

Lance's private anger has cooled. I think he felt sorry for me when I resorted to tears, a weapon that sparingly can be used to great effect. I know Eva has had to surmount much in her life and has played her miserable hand brilliantly, but so have I. Haven't I surmounted great obstacles to arrive where I am now? Isn't that worth anything? Don't I deserve a modicum of respect? He lies in bed with me as if afraid to touch me, though I am hoping for consolation and forgiveness. His arms are raised and folded under his head. He is struggling, I think, for the words that will leave no room for misunderstanding. "There is no comparison," he says, "between your life and hers."

As I slide my hand over his belly and into his groin, hoping to spark a little fire, a warmth of forgiveness, I am intoxicated by the smells of his body. I move my face into the pit of his arm as if it were a cup of ambrosia from which I take a deep, solemn drink. He remains unmoved, although I know he is not sleeping.

Lavrentii Jr. Speaks

In June 1987, I went to Mirgorod. This is how it transpired.

In February, I talk to my parents. "I want to visit our family."

"You are visiting your family. You are home." My mother looks up from her book as if there is something she has misheard.

"I want to go to Mirgorod."

There is silence. Then she asks, "Why? There is no one left."

"What about your brother?"

"Dead."

"Your mother?"

"Dead."

"Your father?"

There is more silence. Then she says, "If he isn't dead by now, he should be."

"I can visit their graves then."

"You'll never find them."

"I'll find the house you lived in. I'll ask questions. People like to talk."

"Who knows if the house is still there?"

She calls Papa in. "Lavr, can you speak to this boy? He has lost his mind." Then she says to me, "Have you lost your mind? This is not a quick trip across the bridge. It is a journey to the other side of the mountain. More like the bottom of the pit. If you get to the bottom, you may never get out."

"Lavrentii, what is this about?" My father has shuffled into the room at last.

Mother is beginning to panic. "Can you speak to your son?"

Papa knows the matter is serious, for otherwise, she never calls for advice or counsel, nor does she call him Lavrentii.

"I want to go to Mirgorod."

"So go. So what's the problem? You need money?" He is unfazed.

"Have you both lost your mind? Lavryushenka, what kind of nonsense is this? You know there is nothing there to see. Go to Moscow. Go to Petersburg. There are museums, palaces, universities, monasteries—isn't that what interests you? What's in Mirgorod? Just dirt and poverty."

"I want to see where you were born and find our relatives."

"I told you I have no relatives. They are dead."

"But your father might still be alive, and if so, I want to meet him."

"And if he is dead, as he should be, what will you do then?"

"Do you know for sure that he died?"

"It doesn't matter whether he is biologically dead or not. You know how I feel."

Papa surprises me. He intervenes. He says if I must go, I should go, and if the relatives are dead, I should pay my respects. I should then see what the Soviets have done with the country. "Perhaps," he continues, "I will be surprised; perhaps you will be surprised; and perhaps even your mother will be surprised."

He looks directly at her. "You cannot stop him," he says matter-of-factly, and he shuffles calmly back out of the room.

The argument went in circles until, suddenly, it stopped. We knew where we stood. Mother said no. I said yes. Papa said to explore. There was little more to say. She would not help me. I would have to do all of my own planning, organization, and research. I was twenty years old, a master of organization and research. All I needed from them was an address. Mother gave it to me grudgingly, but she gave it. What money I needed for research would be supplied by the university, and finances for my personal detour of discovery would be complemented by cash generously provided, of course, by my father. Papa would make sure I could not be stranded in a country too close to the bone to trust.

In 1987, Perestroika had not yet carved up the Union and sent the republics tumbling back into the third world or clawing to remain barely in the second. Language would not be a problem, nor would money. I was interested not just for the sake of my own history but also for academic reasons. I had been in Moscow and Kiev two years before, visiting monasteries. The subject of Mirgorod never came up. I should have found it strange at that time that I was not encouraged to go or that there was no discussion around the possibility of my going. Likely, the subject was judiciously avoided. With Moscow and Kiev, I had my agenda. Frankly, stopping in Mirgorod did not occur to me then. When I was a boy, after church one day, Branka described Mirgorod in Poltava Province to me. She said that you could grow anything on the land. She told me that after it had been overrun by the soldiers, they—meaning she, my mother, and other young girls like them—were sent off to work in factories in Germany. She said Germans needed free or cheap labor for the war effort in order to build guns. The young girls had no choice in the matter. "We were slaves," she said, "we young girls who were chosen."

* * *

It is June. Flying over Kiev, I feel like a time traveler, an innocent visitor of a twilight zone, entering a cloud to emerge in an alien universe. Nothing is as expected. Less could be imagined.

I am traveling by bus to an address I have rewritten neatly in my pocket notebook—my mother's scribbles would have been impossible to decipher. The small bus is World War II vintage and rusted over; it has no suspension but is uncluttered and seemingly clean. All surfaces, inside and outside, have a patina of dusty gray with a matte finish that only the passage of time is capable of achieving. Despite the motley colors and confused combinations of women's and children's dresses on display nearly everywhere, drabness seems to be a fact of life here. It is hot on this early summer day. All of the windows of the bus are open, although it is clearly indicated along the top of the glass panes that they must remain closed while the bus is in motion. So much for rules. The passengers pretend not to notice a young man with a backpack, but they are acutely aware of my every movement—as I am of their curiosity—as they turn their heads while I remove money from my pocket and count it out for the collector. Some never make eye contact. Others stare at the young man from elsewhere. It feels much like curiosity tempered with disdain. The bus driver calls out my stop but barely looks at me as I thank him on the way down and out the door.

* * *

There are not many street signs. A man at the bus station told me it was about a fifteen-minute walk back from the stop, which is located on the corner. But as I look around, I am confused and unable to decipher which direction to travel. A babushka with a basket of green beans and eggs sits at the shaded stop across the street.

"Excuse me, please. Can you direct me to Uspenskaya Ulitza?"

She is at first wary of my strange appearance, but when I smile, she returns the gesture, and I notice her shiny gold teeth—two on the top left and three on the bottom, giving imbalance to an otherwise-symmetrical round face with kind, doughy features. But she seems to know where the street called Uspenskaya is, and her directions prove to be impeccable. I am to travel straight back in the direction I came, and at the house with yellow and blue irises—she uses the word *petushki*, a word my mother used, which, in Russian, means "roosters" as well as "flowers"—I am to turn left and travel another seven minutes or so past three or four streets before taking a final left onto Uspenskaya.

"Who are you looking for?" she asks me.

"Konstantin Korolenko."

"Oh yes," she says kindly, "he will be happy to see you."

"Do you know him?"

"No. Not personally. But I have heard of him."

"How will he know I am coming? I have not written."

"We're always happy to have visitors from somewhere else. How long will you stay?"

"I don't know. I have never met him before. Perhaps just for tea." I surprise myself that I am so forthcoming with a person I have just met. I am not my usual self here.

"For tea? Ridiculous! You should stay for several days. He will be sweeping the ground below your feet."

* * *

On Uspenskaya, I walk past several houses surrounded by high fences, most in a state of disrepair. I manage to walk past the house I am looking for, because there are no numbers on the doors. I come to another house with two women standing at the front gate. One is eating sunflower seeds—pealing them in her mouth and spitting out the shells while she talks. As I walk past, both women stop and stare directly.

"Whose house are you looking for?"

"Konstantin Korolenko's house."

The one hulling sunflower seeds smiles and indicates with her finger I must retrace my steps. I have come too far. "It is the white one with a brown gate," she tells me. Now it is my turn to stare. She notices. I am struck by the astounding resemblance of this woman to Mama; she has a narrow gap between her two front teeth, a preternatural squint to her eyes, and soft, aging blonde hair. It's as if she and my mother were cast from the same iron, members of the same tribe. The other one flashes a mouth full of gold. She seems younger than the first and far too young for such a baroque display of dental work. I thank them as I turn around, hoping my staring has not turned my surprise into spectacle.

I approach the house slowly. The front yard is bare of flowers or bushes but is neat and clean. It is apparent that someone lives here and regularly tends the property. As I remove my camera from my sack and prepare to take a picture, the front door opens. A once-tall but now severely bent and bespectacled old man emerges.

"*Da? Khto ty?* Yes? Who are you?" There is no ceremony here. The old man's voice is jagged and hard.

"*Zdravctvuyete.* Hello!" I try to be bright. "My name is Lavrentii Veronin; my mother is Eva Konstantinovna Veronina." I say the names the Russian way, with patronymic included and agreeing endings. "Her name was Korolenko before she married the first time. I believe this is the house where she once lived. I am looking for Konstantin Korolenko."

The old man, squinting as if to see better and pursing his lips as if to measure out words that do not come, stands silent for what seems an ocean of time.

"*Podkhody.* Approach." He softens, motioning with his hand.

"May I take this picture first?" Perhaps this is a way for me to prepare for my encounter and to buffer the shock for him and for me as well. I take shots from several angles, managing to include this incredulous old man staring directly into the camera at the edge of each frame. When finished, I approach.

"Where have you come from?" he asks.

When I tell him, he seems familiar with my address, repeating several times a word that does not roll easily off the tongue here. "Massachusetts." He has practiced this word before. I am sure of it.

"*Zakhody.* Enter." He holds the door for me, offers to take my backpack, and then pulls out a chair for me at the table. "I am Konstantin Sergeyevich Korolenko. You are Eva's son," he says at last, quietly, in a deep voice, scratched by miles of nicotine.

"Yes."

He stands for a few moments as if in a trance, nodding his head, looking at me, through me, and beyond.

"Tea?"

"Please. May I help?"

"Sit. Rest."

He slowly gathers cups from an open cupboard, places them on the table, and then returns to the sink to fill up the kettle.

There is an ashtray full of cigarette butts next to two open books on a table near a window. Injunctions against the dangers of smoking do not seem to have made it to this distant corner of the world, so they are of little consequence here. On the other hand, this man has survived into his eighties, I am sure. The house carries deep in its pores the layered smells of stale and recently burned tobacco as well as the sourness of kraut or pickling mixed with freshly boiling cabbage on the stove. The stench of onions adds to the potpourri of pungent odors. The smells remind me of postchurch lunches.

"*Stopochku?*" he asks me. I presume he is offering vodka or some local hooch. He pulls a bottle of clear spirit with no label from a shelf and places it in the center of the table.

"No. Thank you."

It is not yet eleven in the morning.

"May I?" He fills his own glass full and drinks it in one gulp. Then he pours himself another and goes off to check the cabbage.

"*Goloden?* Are you hungry?"

"I could eat a little. But right now, a cup of tea would be perfect."

"Hmm." He nods and continues to look at me. I am certain he wants to talk but does not know how or where to begin. Perhaps I shall help him.

"My mother, Eva, wrote the address for me. I should have written to you before coming. I'm sorry I didn't. This is probably too disruptive for you."

"It's nothing. It doesn't matter. I am glad you are here." He picks up the cups, shuffles back over to the stove, prepares the tea, and carefully, with trembling hands, sets both cups on the table.

"Sugar?" he asks while setting out what looks like white rock candy. I thank him.

He stacks the two open books on top of one another and pushes them to the side of the table. I easily catch *Barbarossa* written in bold Cyrillic on the spine of one of them. He pulls out another cigarette, lights it, inhales deeply, and drinks the second glass of spirit.

I ask him what he is reading.

"More lies, more fantasy, junk," he answers. I have noticed that both titles invoke the war.

"How is my Yevochka?"

He seems calmer now. "She is fine."

I pull out a folder with pictures of Mama and Papa. "These were taken a year or so ago," I tell him. In the photo, they have come to see me get an award, although I keep that to myself. They are smiling into the camera.

"This is your father?" he asks. "Nice-looking man. My Yevochka looks elegant. She must be about sixty in this picture. She looks well." He touches her face. "She has changed. She has put on weight. *Nu, da*," he adds. "You can't look like a girl forever."

He looks up and stares at me. "You resemble your father, but you have your mother's eyes. I don't remember—were they brown or blue?"

"Blue."

"How old are you?"

"I will be twenty on my next birthday in November."

"My son, your uncle Il'ko, was born in November but didn't make it to his twentieth birthday."

"I'm sorry." There is silence, and then I ask, "How did he die?"

"He was shot during the war with the Fascisti. Executed."

"I'm sorry." I say it again and take a sip of my tea as he gulps down another glass of alcohol. He drains the remainder of the bottle into his glass, gets up, and mixes the soup. He stands mixing for a bit longer than necessary, wipes his face with his sleeve, pulls hard on his cigarette, brushes away the ash that has fallen onto his shirt, and sits down again. "It's nothing," he says as I stare at the stain left by the cigarette. I presume he means the ash.

"It happened a long time ago. Before you were born."

There is more silence.

"Il'ko was a golden boy. *Zolotoy*."

His cough gurgles up from deep within his chest like the unhurried eruption of a volcano. He pulls a gray handkerchief from his pocket and spits into it. He wipes his face, blows his nose, puts back the soiled handkerchief, sits down again, and cleans his glasses with a soft towel hanging on the back of the chair.

"It was horrible. The Fascisti were everywhere then. First they took our Yids, then our sons, and then our daughters." He uses the pejorative, *Zhidi*, instead of the sanitized version of *Yevrei*. I feel a twinge of disgust. I hope I have not stepped into the mouth of a beast.

He finally snuffs out the cigarette, which he has smoked down to his bony fingers.

He is offering information I do not ask for. It is clear he has thought about this for a long time.

"And what about Babushka? Perhaps I can visit her grave?" I attempt to change the subject.

"Of course," he says. "It is not far from here. Let's eat a little something first."

He rises to bring some plates, but as if to change his mind, he looks over at me and asks if I would like to see Yevochka's room.

"We kept it ready for her. We thought she would come home. Many of the girls did, you know."

"Of course," I stammer.

At least forty years have passed since she has lived here. I do not expect to see much evidence of my mother's life in this room.

"My wife, Zinaida, kept it clean. My woman comes several times a week—keeps it neat for me." He says this as we amble over to the door at the end of a short corridor. I wonder what he means by "my woman." As I look inside, I strain to see signs of my mother as a girl. The bed is covered by a white crocheted bedspread, which I touch with my hand. It is not the kind of quaint ornateness my mother would have ever chosen for herself; I am sure of it.

"Zina made it—crocheted it square by square. She wanted to give it to her when she came back to visit. She made one for Il'ko too."

"Beautiful," I tell him. I also notice the pillows with the famous Slavic cross-stitch. I remember similar work from Branka's house, although it was absent from ours. It does not occur to me until now that we should have had something like this in our house as well. Displays of such craft were everywhere in the church I used to visit before my mother went agnostic on us.

The walls are bare in Eva's room, but a small picture on her dresser table cries out for viewing. Eva is young. She is a teenager, yet she does not appear insolent or deliberate. She is squinting into the sunlight with her hand shielding her eyes from the glare. Can she ever have been so innocent?

"She seems very happy here," I tell him.

"Those were happier days." His cough erupts again suddenly, as if out of nowhere.

Time lives in a bubble here. It exists without spoken language, and without beginning or end, it forms under an umbrella of characters who coexist simultaneously, drifting and dropping in and out of the old man's mind like specters in an infinite loop. My mother seems to have deprived this circle of connections with the necessary switch, the interruption capable of giving form to the circle's history, or at least chronology to its shameful parade of events. Most lives here in this land of disappeared and disappearing are like this. Hardly an hour has gone by, yet this man's life has replayed like a song. It will repeat until the only off button silences the entire apparatus forever.

* * *

We sit down to eat our soup. *Shchi*, he calls it—a kind of cabbage borscht. It smells surprisingly good, and I am hungry, although my stomach seems to be battling nervousness. He shuffles slowly into a pantry and returns with a loaf of hard brown rye bread and a plate full of butter. He grabs a large knife and, holding the bread to his chest while cutting toward himself, produces several uneven slices. I wince at the thought of a stray cut drawing blood. "Don't worry. I'm used to this. Never cut myself," he says. He places the slices directly on the table, along with the remainder of the loaf.

"Take some bread and butter," he urges. "It is very good with the soup."

"How did Babushka Zina die?" I know my mother will ask me when I return, and I am curious.

"Cancer. Lung cancer."

"Did she smoke too?"

"Never. You would expect me to be the one to die, no?"

I am not sure whether it is polite to smile. "It is strange, though. Isn't it?"

"Maybe it is my punishment. After all, it is easier for her now than for me."

"Branka told me that things happen for a reason. When I was a little boy, that is, she told me—"

"What reason?" he sputters. "Things just happen. Reason has nothing to do with it."

The old man begins to cradle the remainder of his cigarette pack in his fingers, as if he is about to light up another one, but then he releases it. Just as abruptly, he turns his head to stare out the window.

"My Zina always thought that Yevochka would come home, even for a visit. Many of our girls living in other countries have come back. She always blamed me. She told me it was my fault."

I don't understand the reference. "Your fault for what?"

"That Eva did not come home. Zina called me a traitor. She called me everything she could think of."

He is about to say something more but thinks better of it. I can hear the two women I met earlier passing slowly outside the window.

"Hello, Konstantin Sergeyevich," sings out my mother's younger clone. He ignores her.

"She never forgave me."

"Forgave you for what?" I am still confused.

He looks down at the soup and goes silent.

Still engrossed in his borscht, he takes a big spoonful and chews it slowly, letting the broth wash down. The heat in the room, made more palpable by the steaming soup, does not seem to disturb this old man, my grandfather. I am sweating.

"Aren't you hot?" I ask.

"Doesn't matter. No."

"How long ago did she die?"

"Ten, eleven, twelve years or so ago. We will see when we go to the graves." He continues slurping his soup with an occasional cough in between. It seems as if the hot soup is clearing his lungs and sinuses and making him stronger. I notice that some color has come into his wizened face. Even his eyes seem to shine more brightly from behind the spectacles.

* * *

"Do you read much?" I ask.

"What else should I do? Sometimes I watch a film." He points to a small TV in another corner of the room, in front of which stands a dirty, dilapidated old chair vaguely brown in color. "I prefer the old Soviet films, the war films. Lots of junk, but they show you how we had to live then."

"You mean when the Fascists were here?"

"And before the Fascisti came, we struggled to survive. They don't teach you that in American universities, do they? Our own leader made a famine in '33 that left millions of people dead. Did you learn that? And when our devil made a pact with the German devil, we were doomed. It was as if we were being devoured from both sides by sharks. Stalin, who trusted nobody, decided to trust

Hitler. And when Hitler betrayed him, his politburo should have shot him dead right there in the Kremlin, where he cowered like a sheep for days. But they were terrified of this sheep—all of them. And they expect bravery from the people? *Yob s'nimi.*" He spits. "Fuck them."

I am taken aback by this rush of fury.

"You know, when Batyushka Stalin died, I took Zina outside and danced a polka with her. Right there in the front yard! No matter what they wrote in their newspapers, it was one of the happiest days of the century. We thought that maybe then Yevochka might come home to us. Even for a visit."

"I did read about the famine. And Mama told me about it too. She said that Il'ko nearly died."

"Ah, yes, she remembered. She was a very young girl."

The tirade brings on a silence as he continues to chew his buttered bread and eat his soup.

I finish the soup and feel surprisingly refreshed as the sweat begins to cool my body. He has opened the front door and created a draft. The two women seem to have disappeared.

"No matter what we did, it was betrayal!" he explodes. "We betrayed to save our families. Instead of saving them, we buried them. There were no good sides then." He points to the books on the table. "Not those books or any others will tell you that. For us then, there was nothing but death and starvation. *Smert' i golodovka.* The ones who weren't eaten by the sharks died of slow poison. They're still dying from it."

As if to underscore the point, his cough takes on a sinister character. I hand him the tea as he chokes on his own spittle. He manages at last to find a small, dry corner of his handkerchief in which to expel the offending slime.

It is time for me, with Western arrogance tempered by youthful ignorance and physical disgust at the sight of his expulsions, to be silent.

* * *

We are on the way to the cemetery. It is not far from the house. We walk past several houses that look much like the one Konstantin lives in—drab and colorful at the same time—and then through a glade of trees. On the other side is a vast field of wildflowers. The old man, for all of his apparent infirmity and despite the heat of afternoon sun, has a steady step. He detours slightly into the field to pick some red wildflowers. I ask him if he would like some help. He motions that he wishes for me to wait. Watching him gather flowers, I, a student of history, sense the veil of sadness that seems to envelop this vast landscape as if by definition. Upon his return, he divides the flowers between us and tells me they are for the graves.

"Zina especially liked these red ones."

"What are they called?"

"*Mak.* Poppy. Il'ko didn't care about the poppies, but he liked poppy bread."

I am transported suddenly to my church days—the smell of the poppy bread, the colorful hard-boiled eggs.

"We will be there soon. You can see it from here." He motions in the direction where vegetation and large stones seem to coexist irregularly. I see small trees, some large stones, an overgrowth of weeds in some areas, and small tables and chairs. If I didn't know better, I might mistake it for a picnic area, although irregularity for this purpose makes the space suspect. On the other hand, neither order nor regularity is common here.

"Zinaida and Il'ko are buried together in a plot not far from the main path."

As we continue down the road, a lively band of small boys walks past us with towels and Styrofoam packing materials.

"Where are they going?"

"There is a small river just beyond the edge of the cemetery on the far side. That is where Yevochka learned to swim. She was one of the first, you know. Never afraid of anything."

"It must be strange to walk by a cemetery whenever you want to go swimming."

"It's nothing. These dead souls are family. Dead souls." He laughs, looking me in the eye, as if he alone understands the joke.

He pauses, remembering something.

"This was a small cemetery when Eva was a little girl. Now it looks like half the country is buried here. Between famines and wars, you wonder that anyone is left. Maybe just old geezers like me, waiting to die."

He starts to laugh but then seems to think better of it. Perhaps he does not want to bring another coughing episode upon himself.

The plot has two small, rectangular stones with the name КОРОЛЕНКО grafted into each. An oval picture of Zinaida as an old lady, encased in transparent plastic which has grown brittle and opaque over the years, is attached to the front of the stone along with her dates. There is no picture of Il'ko under his name, but the dates show he had not reached twenty when he died. In front of the stones, there appears to be a flower bed, but nothing is planted. I see only remnants of other flowers strewn across the top. Konstantin clears the dead flowers, pulls a few weeds, and collects cigarette wrappings and other random papers scattered over this small, contained area. He then lays out his poppies and gestures to me to do the same. Around the actual grave, the plot is a stoned-in resting area, but there is not a stool or bench, as I see at other graves.

"Why are there benches and stools there?" I point to several plots around us.

"So people can rest and talk to their dead. I can talk standing up. If you want to sit, just borrow that chair."

"No, this is fine. It was just a question. I am not tired."

I have seen this before. Slavic cemeteries make demands upon the living, reminding them of the spiritual and physical obligations toward their departed. When you are dead, it is up to the living to look after your remains. Perhaps the continued interaction forces a conversation, revisits unresolved conflicts, and prevents amnesia, at least for the living. Guilt, anger, and misunderstanding linger in the air. *A definition of love? A source of family loyalty? This is a strange world,* I think. But who am I to know or understand the historic undercurrents that have shaped this old man's sense of himself?

Some plots contain fruit trees: pears, apples, and sometimes a random fig tree. Some headstones bear graphic portraits of their loved ones, and a few of the largest ones have full-body representations, perhaps copied from pictures. The atmosphere seems to say the dead are still with us instead of suggesting, as we do in the West, that they have moved on to a better place. For the dead, here is the better place, because they do not have to talk to anyone or explain themselves in any way. It is up to the living to conjure worlds around these silent, sparring partners departed in body only.

"How often do you come here?"

"Once a week. Today is special. Zina will meet her grandson, and Il'ko his nephew. Otherwise, it is too hard. Too many recriminations."

I wonder who is recriminating against whom and for what. This old man's punishment seems the only thing keeping him alive—another reversal in this topsy-turvy world.

He pulls another cigarette from his pocket, lights it, takes a deep drag on it, and turns to his wife.

"*Nu*, Zina. *Goct'. Tvoi Vnuk*. Well, Zina, you have a visitor. It is your grandson. From Massachusetts. Eva's son, Lavrentii."

As if she has answered him, he laughs hard enough to cough and expel more mucus. He spits to the side.

"Take a look at your grandson, a tall and handsome young man. Look at his face. He has Eva's eyes."

Zina must be speaking to him, because he is shaking his head while smiling and smoking the cigarette into a breeze wafting its way in my direction. I move a bit to his left to avoid the acrid exhaust assaulting my nostrils. My sneeze alerts him to my whereabouts. He turns and looks at me for a moment before replying to a question from his ghosts. "Yes, of course, I am taking good care of him."

Perhaps in death, Zina has told him all of the things she kept to herself when alive. It is no wonder he comes here often.

As if prodded by an inaudible voice, he turns again to me and asks, "Why didn't she come back to visit? When you were younger. When Zina was still alive."

"I don't know." It is the truth.

"Eva didn't forgive me, did she?" He turns his head to look down again at Zina's portrait in plastic, but he is addressing me. "I would have been able to explain to her. Maybe she would have understood. And if not, at least I would have tried. At least her mother would have seen her again."

He sputters as if he is on the verge of unleashing a volcanic sob but pulls hard again on the cigarette, regaining composure.

"We thought at first the Fascisti would rescue us. Can you imagine how stupid we were?"

His laugh reminds me somewhat of my mother's. It emerges as a mercy, brittle and hard for a bitter lesson learned too late.

"It must have been very hard during the war." I am almost ashamed of my cliché-ridden comments.

"It was hell before the war, it was hell during the war, and it was hell right after. It is still hell. First, Stalin tried to starve us to death, and then Stalin and the Fascisti tried to shoot us to death. After the war, it was all we could do to bury our dead and count our losses. Il'ko did not deserve to die. He wasn't yet even a man." At this, he touches the gravestone and runs his fingers across his son's name.

"Zina's words dried up. She stopped talking. No words, no looks, no cooking, no cleaning. For months that stretched maybe into years. Even before she died, she was dead. My Zinochka."

"The Fascists were brutal," I say. It is another weary observation from a child of plenty.

"The Fascisti were brutal, but Il'ko didn't die by a German bullet. He joined the Soviets and then was taken prisoner by the Germans. About three miles from here. But when the prisons were liberated, half the prisoners were marched out by their own troops, their liberators." He spits out the words with biting scorn. "And they were shot. The NKVD called them traitors because they were stupid enough to be captured." He pauses to take another long drag on the cigarette, which, by this time, has burned down to his fingers. He abruptly throws down the remains of the butt.

"I ask you: What country kills its own soldiers?" He looks at me but does not expect an answer. He has grappled with this question many times before. "The Fascisti carried off our Jews; the Soviets finished off the rest of us.

"You are a handsome young man—intelligent and lucky. Nothing is simple. My history books make the past look organized and logical, a battle between the good and the very bad. It's all nonsense! Pure shit. I read only the books about this history. But none of them tells you the true story. They just organize facts, assemble theories, and glorify their own actions. Me? I tried to buy one child with another and lost them both. My wife never stopped hating me for it."

I can think of nothing pithy to ease this old man's agitation. He leans against his wife's stone to rest and draw a breath of natural air for a change. He is, for a short moment, without nicotine. It is not long before he straightens enough to pull a last cigarette from the crumpled package, which he then banishes to the side of the plot. With his trembling fingers, he hands me the matches and asks me to light the last one. He looks at me and laughs. I notice a lower jaw of small nicotine-colored teeth that have, over the years, strayed far from their original design yet remained devoid of any gold substitutions.

* * *

On the way home, he trudges with short but definite steps. He manages to kick away empty beer bottles impeding the way. "Hooligans," he repeatedly mutters. As he does this, I begin to perceive the broken alcohol bottles randomly strewn along the roads and pathways that have led me here. He goes silent until we pass a modest house that appears to be abandoned. He points out this house as the one where Branka's family lived. When I approach it to attempt a peek over the fence, I am nearly assaulted by a large, snarling Alsatian shepherd that beats up against a tall, dilapidated wooden fence like the ones I have seen all over. "Careful," the old man warns, almost too late. "The dog is vicious."

"The house looks empty," I say, attempting to hide my fright.

He tries to reassure me, gently pulling on my arm, a gesture meant to calm me and keep me out of harm's way, while the hound repeatedly lunges against the fence from the inside.

"It is, but a man who lives in the center of Mirgorod will repair it for his daughter. She is getting married next year. The dog protects against the hooligans." He means those who have painted the landscape with their own version of colorful trash.

"Do you remember Branka well?" I am still confused in trying to build a chronology of events.

"Of course. They were inseparable as young girls. They were both carted off to Germany."

We continue walking for a while without exchanging words. He seems to drift in and out of his thoughts back to where I am watching and waiting for another syllable of information that will confer knowledge or understanding on our dark histories. I feel there will be many more questions after my visit. I think I am just beginning to understand why Mother spoke so little of her time here. I wonder how to confront her with questions she will not wish to answer. Perhaps there will be no more to this story than what I learn here.

His eyes have glazed over. He pulls out his handkerchief and blows his nose. He coughs deeply once and spits again to the side. "Branka came to visit us several times while her mother was alive, before my Zina died. Eva sent a letter through her to Zina. How do you think I know so much about you, my grandson from Massachusetts? Every night, I used to read the letter, starting with the address, to Zina as if it was a bedtime story. It was the only thing that could put a smile on her face. The grandson from Massachusetts."

"I didn't know Mother wrote."

"What? She didn't tell you about us?"

"Yes, of course. A little," I lie.

"Just a little, eh? Yes, indeed, she wrote. I know the letter by heart."

* * *

By the time we have arrived back at the house, I am exhausted, as much from the excursion as from the strange talks between the living and dead.

I ask tentatively, "Why have Mother and Zina never forgiven you?"

"Because I thought I could outsmart the devil."

"Which devil?"

"Both. Either."

"I mean, what happened?"

There is silence.

He removes his spectacles for a moment, moves to the sink, and allows water to run over them. He dries them slowly with what appears to be the only clean dishtowel, replaces them, and sits down again. He stares at me and repeats that I am an intelligent and lucky young man.

He stands up again and puts on the kettle for some hot water. "Let's drink some tea," he says as he opens another cupboard. I expect he is looking for tea, biscuits, or the like. Instead, he reaches for another bottle of clear spirit and another fresh pack of cigarettes. It has been a quarter of an hour since he has had a cigarette—the time it takes for the old man to walk from Branka's old house to his home. He struggles to open the bottle; after succeeding, he places it in the middle of the table, next to the history books, which, in silent reproach, have not moved since he pushed them aside. He reaches for a cup and places it in front of me. For himself, he grabs a tall glass and pours it nearly full of his spirit, which he drinks down in several gulps. He hands me the cigarette package and asks me to open it; he says it takes him longer to open the package than to smoke one of its cigarettes. Thanking me, he extracts one and lights it. Drawing long and hard, he appears to be pondering a response to my question.

"Eva was a remarkable girl. Even in this forsaken village, she stood out. When she was fifteen or sixteen, maybe seventeen, she ran away from home with a boy from the market—a Jew. When she came back several days later, she looked like she had been dragged through dirt. Sleeping in caves in the woods, alone like an animal. She told her mother she wanted to die. *Dura.* Foolish girl. For months, she was not the same. Her schoolwork suffered; she became disrespectful—toward her mother but especially toward me. She hated me then. Yes, I know girls of that age give their parents difficulty, but this was something different. Much worse."

"Did you reprimand her?" I expect, in vain, some sign of an enlightened approach to difficult behavior.

"Of course I reprimanded her! As I should have done! I knew what happened. When he was done with her, he just left her in the dirt. This stupid, stupid girl.

"When the Fascisti came, we thought we were being liberated. It took no time to understand who they really were, and maybe it was too late already for my Il'ko, who managed to get himself thrown into one of their jails. I don't understand why they didn't shoot him at once. They were shooting everyone else. Maybe they wanted information from him. Maybe they thought of him as just another snot-nosed kid. I don't know. This mystery I have grappled with for half a lifetime.

"Zina was terrified. She begged me to go to them, to plead for his life."

There is another long pause in which he attempts to gather strength for the journey back into his past.

"Did you go?" I try to help him along.

"Of course I went. He was my son. Zina was mad with worry."

"What did you say to them?"

"I offered them information."

Suddenly, I am afraid of going another step forward. I realize I have just placed my foot on the edge of the abyss.

He proceeds, now more steadily. "I told them my daughter had information."

"What kind of information?"

"That she might know where people were hiding."

Sometimes just a misplaced word, a revealing movement of another's head, or a sudden shifting of another's eyes can turn the universe on its head and change its appearance forever. Your world implodes, and the estimation of your personal courage shrivels up like burned leaves. Up becomes down, down becomes up, white becomes black or gray, and good—or the idea of it—disappears into an infinity of absurdities never to be heard from again. You suddenly realize that misunderstanding rules the order of events, while clarity is a figment of imagination. "Loss of innocence" is inadequate to describe such an assault on the mind. As these moments become unbearable, I feel all of these things at once.

Konstantin must have sensed my discomfort. I think he feels he doesn't need to or can't say any more. I am glad. He finishes his cigarette in silence; walks over to the sink, coughing again; turns on the spout; and expunges a stream of mucus. He watches the water wash away these emanations of his body, as if by doing so, the water can render him cleansed of impurity and absolved of transgression. At that moment, I cannot judge him more harshly than I believe he has judged himself.

"When you play with the devil, the devil always wins. Even when he loses, he wins." These are his last words to me on this subject.

* * *

"I think it is time for me to start getting back to the hotel," I tell him. "It will take me just over an hour to return to the station and then another quarter hour to reach my hotel." My watch reads a few minutes after four o'clock.

"Yes." He nods quietly. "I understand."

He removes his glasses, places them gently on his history books, and wipes his face with another clean towel, which he has pulled from a small cupboard next to the sink. He seems suddenly exhausted. He slouches into the chair, letting his long arms hang down nearly to the floor. I realize how tall and slender he must have been in his youth. Mother once said her father was proud of the way he spoke, a kind of high Russian among the peasants, and the way he was able to write sentences of elegant prose in beautifully legible script. She told me that as a young father, he used to lift her to his shoulders and walk through the neighborhood. She told me that from where she sat, the ground seemed far away, but she was never frightened. He held her tightly with one hand while he smoked his cigarettes with the other. Always, he reassured her, she could not fall. Long ago, she told me this was one of her first memories from childhood.

"*Pora*. It is time," I say, rising from my chair and moving to retrieve my backpack from the small divan in the corner of the room.

"*Da, pora.* Yes, it is time," he answers, standing up and replacing his spectacles. "Shall I walk with you to the bus stop?"

"You must be very tired."

"Just a little."

"Thank you."

"It is I who should be thanking you. Thank you. I only wish you could have come sooner. Next time—if you ever come again, that is—you'll find me under a rock at the place we visited today." He laughs again in the familiar way, dry and brittle.

He takes my arm as if to lead me out but stops abruptly just before opening the door. He excuses himself, telling me to wait. "I'll be right back," he promises, shuffling back into the room at the end of the short corridor. From where I stand, his breathing seems more labored; the heavy wheeze is more audible. He is working hard and seems to be conversing with phantoms. Several times, I clearly hear the name Zina or Zinochka. I smile, thinking I have discovered the source of one of my mother's strange habits.

When he comes back out, he is carrying the white crocheted bedspread folded neatly in his arms.

"This is for your mother. Zina meant to give it to her, but she couldn't wait long enough. Put it in your pack. It's not very heavy."

"I can't take this," I protest foolishly. "It is too beautiful."

"You don't understand. You must take it. Zina insists. Besides, you are young and strong." He laughs, as if sensing my reservations about its weight. There will be no more argument.

The bus, after taking many turns, eventually arrives on a straight road heading into the city center. There is an empty beer bottle rolling along the floor every which way like an apple bobbing on water, the hapless refuse of one of the ubiquitous hooligans caught in this place and time. It has appeared as if out of nowhere, perhaps dislodged by the earlier sometimes-violent turns of the bus. We travel through green landscapes made more vivid by heavy precipitation in the air. It looks like rain. My mind returns to the vast cemetery surrounded by red poppies, where the remaining inhabitants of this land, with its painful history, go to meet their dead, brush off their stones, and weed their small, enclosed flower beds. Each day, they rise to meet the light, as they have done for centuries, opening their eyes and preparing to just go on.

* * *

This is how the visit to my grandfather transpired.

Part II: Sugar

Eva

Mercy was not at breakfast this morning, which passed without incident. There were no grizzly theatrics with cinnamon toast, thank goodness. The tone is now civil and high-minded. We discuss my poets: Akhmatova, who suffered for love and politics, and Mandelstam, who lost his teeth and died mad as a hatter in one of the gulags. "Political systems are not mean," Lavrentii argues, "just fragile."

"Fragile while wielding a hammer and a gun?" I ask.

"Meanness has nothing to do with it." He remembers what his father used to say: "Politics is easy. Economics is easy. Until, that is, you inject people into the equations."

"But isn't that the point?" I counter. "We create these systems for people, not in spite of them. More likely, these architects of a better world see their own well-being as paramount. Who will carry out the great work if the clear thinkers are not allowed by the muddled hotheads to prevail?"

Lavrentii understands I am being ironic. He and I agree, I think, on the nature of political action, neither of us believing in the pristine purity of motive. I think this is so in most areas of human affairs. Pardon the pun. From what I have read, Buddha and Jesus might be the exceptions, although I can easily be persuaded otherwise.

Lavinia is subdued. Whether because of yesterday's incident or the topic to which we are always returning—the demons and heroes of our big war—I cannot tell. She doesn't usually participate in discussions unless the subject is science or medicine. Then we troglodytes are expected to listen rapturously and accept her pronouncements as gospel. She is indeed our resident expert in these areas. But in fairness, when Lavrentii and I become embroiled in these discourses, she listens attentively and usually asks relevant questions. But today, as the discussion degenerates into another diatribe against the glorious five-year plans to save the cities from hunger, with Lavrentii complacently agreeing that they indeed wrought horrors, Lavinia seems preoccupied, even uninterested, playing with her yogurt and cereal like a child. I wonder why I need to pay so much attention to her moods. "Where's Mercy?" I ask her, knowing from having missed the morning chirpings that Mercy is nowhere in the house now. "Is she swimming with Maribel?"

Lavinia explains, without looking up at me, still stirring her yogurt, that Mercy is at a sleepover with her girlfriends. "What girlfriends? Maribel? We don't know anyone else here," I say. There is no hostility in my voice, and I fight to keep from showing my disappointment. I wonder out loud how many nights she will be away. This time, I ask Lavrentii. He tells me she is returning after lunch. He acts peculiarly, though. He seems to tread gingerly and would rather lie to his mother than upset his wife any more than she is already upset.

I have heard them whispering to one another. This morning, Lavinia's eyes were red and slightly swollen. I saw him consoling her after she returned from her morning sun ritual and swim, which seemed longer today than usual. He swept the hair from her face and tenderly placed two kisses on each eyelid. With his right hand, he brushed away some particle, a dried salt crystal or a grain of sand perhaps, from the corner of her eye. Then he wrapped his arms around her and held her without saying a word. I have always suspected her to be damaged goods, no matter how accomplished she is. I do not doubt that she has climbed mountains of garbage to get where she is. She remains, nonetheless, frail, fractured, and undermined from within. On the other hand, perhaps I am imagining everything.

But to her, I am infinitely grateful for Mercy.

* * *

It is late afternoon, and I am still waiting for Mercy. I have taken my shot, in the thigh this time. Lavrentii is at least gentle. He is torn between his wife and his mother. He suffers not least because he implodes.

I have slept a bit after reading Akhmatova's poem over and over again: "I have learned to live simply and humbly / To look at the sky and pray to God." I am not being facetious.

It is unlike Mercy to avoid her grandmother. She will usually bounce in to say hello or to make a date for our late-morning visit or afternoon talk. I have never depended on anyone, but for her, I wait and wait, and when she arrives, I treasure every second, hang on every word, and notice every gesture. Curious, isn't it? Is it possible she is dearer to me than was Lavrentii at that age? A grandmother's prerogative is to favor whomever she pleases. Lavrentii claims she had an invitation. He'll say and do anything to maintain the peace. I nearly asked whether her mother is having her conversations taped but caught myself in the nick of time. "Disappointment brings on a fit of disagreeable pique that it is in my power to control," I tell myself, muttering under my breath. Instead, I ask him to turn on the TV. In this modern world of personal exploration, the likes of Oprah have replaced Akhmatova. Instead of poetry, daily blather grinds substance to an easily digestible mush. Some fool on the screen is expressing love by leaping on the couch. So this is how it is done these days?

I am afraid that if Lavinia knows I miss Mercy so much, she will use it against me—if not this time, then next. I continue to hedge my bets—isn't that what they say in English?—by behaving in a stellar manner: "Yes, dear. Of course, dear. Not at all, dear."

* * *

I am suddenly overcome with an unbearable desire for sweetness—sugar, plain and simple. Compensation, Lavinia and her professional friends would call it—a kind of aphrodisiac for the twilight people who can barely make it to the toilet on time. *Give an old woman who will not be a burden much longer a bit of sugar to accelerate the process. If no Mercy, then let me eat sugar, and I will no longer be an albatross around your necks. Simple terms. You don't expect me to believe that nonsense about the Hippocratic oath.*

Doctors are people just like everyone else. They let other people die all the time if it will save them a headache. They murder with the best and the worst of intentions. I read about a Wellesley doctor who bludgeoned his wife while they were walking their dog around the pond. He probably got tired of her when she became menopausal. I bet he sought out whores from the Internet. If Lavrentii's father had ever done that to me, I'd have pushed him out the door in an instant. "You want whores? Go. Be happy," I would have said. As if tricks can make you happy.

Just a cookie. Just one goddamn cookie! An Oreo for the soul. How demeaning that the life of this old lady is reduced to the pursuit of unhealthy dessert. This is the time I should be watching my life flash before me, assembling the facts, and regretting the failures. Without regret, there is no enlightenment. Better late! Instead, I am licking my lips and salivating for junk food. What a mockery of the human condition. Who cares about dignity or enlightened old age? Goodness, why do they deprive me of Mercy? Because I crave cinnamon and sugar? Because the child is beginning to understand the chicanery of adults? Can they really believe that I, the babushka who loves Mercy more than life, am the instrument of her corruption? And if so, so what? What is education if not corruption? Corruption gets a bad reputation. Sometimes it is the difference between survival and demise. The world moves as soon we begin to recognize the people in it. How well we see determines how well we fare. Doesn't that kind of corruption improve vision and increase strength? Or not?

Residual heat, despite the coolness of the ocean, makes my head swim. I tire easily at this time of day.

* * *

"Guten Morgen. Is Eva here?" He has asked in a tone that could not be misunderstood as anything but imperious.

Yet Mother dares a "Why Eva?" before this strapping officer with the shiny white skin and the blue eyes. When she calls to me, I hear the terror in the trill of her voice. How does he know my name, this beautiful intruder? We make ready to march. He places his gloved hand firmly on her chest to bid her away when she begs to follow. In his perfect Russian, he assures her of my safety. "*Pozhaluysta,*" he says. "Please." It is not a request.

He lifts me easily into the jeep while one of the soldiers climbs behind the wheel. The others arrange themselves respectfully in the remaining seats. While holding me tightly, he places my hand on his knee and begins to pet it with his gloved hand. I am afraid to look up, but I somehow know he is looking hard at me and smiling. This road is a familiar one, though it looks different in autumn daylight. The sun is beginning to warm the air, although it makes no difference to me. My body, convulsing with terror or cold, takes no comfort in its warmth. I do not recall how long or where we ride, but suddenly, as if by an instinct or a residual memory of time and distance, I look up to recognize the spot of the donkey and the rainbow, and I abruptly turn in the direction of the hollow on the opposite side of the road. By the time I have caught myself, it is too late. The officer has stopped the car and is leading me in the direction where it all began for me—toward the hollow, toward paradise, toward hell, toward my damnation.

We are walking steadily. The officer is clutching my wrist as if it is a rope that will save him from a ravine, although I am the one who needs saving. I do not remember what we see along the way, because I am looking down at my slippered feet, which push through leaves and rubble as we walk. The crackle is of things breaking—twigs like fingers, leaves like hearts, and lives like playthings of the powerful, I think. He is pulling me, although I think I am expected to be leading him. Two soldiers walk next to me with several others behind. I do not see them, but I can smell their polished boots. It is the smell of chemicals and oil, foreign in this wood, as are the soldiers themselves. It must be autumn, for the colors of the ground are yellow and brown, and there is the smell of burning firewood in the air. I am shivering from the morning cold, yet I continue to drag along the ground the shawl Mother threw at me before I was escorted away.

The morning is crisp, and no wind blows. I can hear the serenade of thrushes in the clearing. They do not comprehend the drama swirling beneath their perches. There is nothing in the air or light to give warning that the sky is falling, that the world will end. My tears are salty, and I am afraid I shall retch. The shivers that shake my body do little to warm it. We walk through brambles and forest thick with once-lush but drying growth and between the small vegetable plots dotted with a few waning tomatoes and cucumbers rotting and gone to seed. The German officer extends his free hand to pat my head as if I am a pet incapable of human grief and unaware of what I am about to do. Do we live so alone in our boxes that we cannot recognize another's terror? When I stop suddenly, he feels the resistance and understands it as a sign that I cannot go another step. The place looks much the same to me as it did on that first morning, but the colors are different. Beguiling greens and yellows have yielded to crisp, drying browns and rotting blacks and purples. My body, no longer my own, begins an inexorable convulsion. It is the place the world first moved for me. I know at this moment my life will be measured from here.

He releases his viselike grip. I turn and run, hoping the soldiers will shoot me. But they do not call after me. They shout neither *"Achtung!"* nor "Halt!" I think they are laughing as if at a stupid and abused animal with burrs in its paws, whose whimpering amuses. As

I run, I lose my slippers, first one and then the other. I do not notice the sharp stones or drying grass that cut into the skin of my soles, nor the branches that whip me as I flee past. "Shoot me. Shoot me," I pray, whispering as I run, for I do not know where I will run to or where I can hide, for there will be no one to comfort me. I pray to Gospodi to let me die like a dog. I am damned like Judas.

My mind registers a sharp popping in the distance, yet I continue to run, praying and cursing, until I can bear it no longer, and then I am gone.

* * *

Suddenly, I am awake and elsewhere. My bed smells clean. The sheets have been dried in the sun, and a freshness invades my nostrils, reminding me of warm spring days, though I somehow know it is autumn. The air is crisp even inside my tiny bedroom streaked with the yellow sun of late afternoon. My eyes register shapes silhouetted against a light that forms a corridor to the open front door. The smell of earth and of frying onions and cabbage mingled with a familiar perspiration belonging to the figure seated on my bed is unmistakable. My feet hurt, though they are clean and warm, now wrapped in towels and tucked neatly under soft covers. Mother seems to blend into the background, where I notice another figure standing erect against the threshold of my room. The caustic odor of Father's cigarette hurts my eyes. "He delivered you here," explains Mother, stroking my face with one rough and calloused hand while genuflecting with the other. "He carried you in. He said you would be fine, better. Two days ago, he said you would get better. 'She will forget everything,' he said."

Who? I wonder, though the answer bursts into my understanding with volcanic fury. She continues. "The officer said you were a good girl. *Poslushnaya* was the word he used. Well behaved."

Father does not utter a word. His shimmering figure at the edges of my waking awareness has dissipated, and where it stood lingers only the smoke from his not-quite-snuffed cigarette. I hear the front door close behind him, and with him, the glare of afternoon sun is gone. I am fully awake now, feeling hollow and coreless yet comforted by the roughness of my mother's tender ministrations. She turns to look in the direction of the door. *"Proklyaty idiot. Damned fool, what could you have been thinking?"* she whispers as she wipes her face with her sleeve. At first, I think she is talking to me, but I see then that her gaze is pointed elsewhere. Her head is turned toward the door; she is staring down at the cigarette slowly smoldering itself into extinction and shaking her head.

Home Again

Mercy did not come for supper today. Lavrentii announced for my edification—I could see from the way he looked me in the eye that he was consoling—that Maribel's mother called. The girls had supper together, they went to the movies, and Mercy will sleep over. I am comfortable that she is safe, and I will see her again soon. After all, she is only visiting at the next house, although for me, it might as well be an ocean away or bordered by a deep ditch. *She'll be back tomorrow.* I think this to myself, but I betray disappointment. A kind of world-weariness encircles me and settles upon me like a suffocating English fog in the old black-and-white Hollywood movies. In my mind, the wet pavement glows diffusely through the mist, and I cannot see the figure that looms ominously before me. *You don't need a team of shrinks to figure that one out,* I tell myself. Lavrentii notices I am gloomy.

"Mother, are you all right?" he whispers, jarring me from my drifting dreams.

"Fine." I try to sound convincing. "I'm very tired," I tell him. "Do I need my shot?" I ask. Lavinia, seated across from me, is still elsewhere in her dreaming. My medical needs seem suddenly unimportant to her. Lavrentii is quite a juggler. He walks me to my room, where I ready myself for the night, and kisses me good night on the forehead.

"*Dobroi Nochi*," he says.

Tender, dear boy of mine. "*Dobroi Nochi*," I answer as if I am saying good-bye and not merely good night. I am able to carry myself from the bathroom to my bed and back despite the heaviness in my limbs.

Nevertheless, I am unable to sleep. Reading again about poor Bazarov, who dies for love or for lack of it, brings on a feverish bout of deep thoughts. My mind races backward and forward in time, but the physical act of tossing and turning is not easy for a woman in my state of decomposition. I am afraid of sores.

* * *

It is 2:17 a.m. I know this because my eyeglasses are still attached to my head, and I can see the hands of the clock on the nightstand next to my bed. Eva, the diabetic, nonperipatetic philosopher, dreamer of lives, fabulist of histories, conjurer par excellence, decides to take a walk without her one disciple, with neither the knowledge nor consent of her handlers. Leaning on her cane, she hauls her abundant derriere from the bed and trudges forward, dragging her body step by heavy step, along a middle corridor, seeking—under the guise of a midnight snack, though it is far past midnight—a wisdom that has always eluded her and a truth whose existence she doubts. Assisted in her endeavor by the repetitive music of the ocean, a reminder at once of the smallness and the bigness of things, she imagines the view from the cosmos. We four-limbed creatures think ourselves so different from one another, but from a spaceship, from other worlds, we behave alike as a unique species made up of subgroups whose differences are negligible from out there. We reproduce and form groups that socialize, argue, fight, and, with amazing mathematical regularity, destroy each other in the cruelest and most creative of ways, though this creativity is hard to measure from space.

Trudging as quietly as possible, I make my way along the corridor leading past the bedrooms and bathroom to the kitchen. It is no mean feat, despite the coolness of the night, for a woman my age with pained feet to play the lithe and quiet thief in a domestic setting. To catch my breath, I stop to rest on my cane in front of their bedroom, where Lavinia's soft and regular snoring attests to the depth of her sleep. Lavrentii, on the other hand, has always been a quiet sleeper. Conveniently locked away in his dreaming, he will not stir even if he hears the rattle of pots or the shattering of glass. It was always that way with him as a child and adolescent, and I assume it to be so now. I move on, reassured. Without help, I feel as if I have hauled a carcass over desert sand, and the momentary rest gives me confidence to move forward toward the pantry of this old cottage, where I am certain to find my gold.

She has hidden a container of Royal Dansk chocolate-chip cookies and a package of Oreos somewhere in this pantry. I am sure of this. I use my pocket light, which I have brought along for the mission, to illuminate the shelves, but at first glance, neither Dansk nor Oreos are anywhere to be seen. I spied them from the window as she was bringing in the groceries this afternoon. I know they are here. She left them carelessly at the top of the bag, visible to wandering, spying eyes like mine. She made a terrible racket in the kitchen while unpacking. I heard the rattling of pots and pans and the slamming of cupboards as she was going about her business. I pretended to sleep but continued listening for clues. *Eva Sherlock!* In the old days, before I came to be as I am today, before the proscription on sugar, I saw her greedily licking the insides of those little black sandwich cookies as if they were caviar. In good humor, I used to chastise my illustrious daughter-in-law for her working-class tastes. Mercy likes them too. *Foolish child.* Lavrentii never touches them. They are just sugar and probably some kind of hydrogenated fat. *Listen to me, will you? I don't even know what hydrogenated fat is. Don't much care either. Look at me. I am a beggar. I'll eat Oreos if I can't find anything else. In fact, I'll eat Oreos no matter what else I find. An Oreo, an Oreo—my meager kingdom, my life for a sweet Oreo cookie.* I have thus reinvented myself for advertising. My muffled laughter sounds much like the braying of an old donkey. I must hold myself in check and steal quietly for the sake of the mission.

Armed with my pocket light in case I need to read in the dark and still wearing my glasses, I undertake the task to find some cookies, no matter how commercial or mundane. I shall not be greedy; I shall eat only one. I promise myself this. They won't notice. If you can forgive a man for pounding his wife of thirty years into oblivion because a genetic trigger has wrought havoc with his physical chemistry, why can't you forgive a simple old woman for wanting to die with pleasure? I am preparing my defense in case I am caught red-handed. Then I'll write to the Hemlock Society: "I want to die of sugar poisoning. Help me." Too bad Dr. Kevorkian is dead.

Suddenly, my incisive detective mind is blessed with a revelation: the pots and pans that behaved so rambunctiously this afternoon live on the shelves of the second inner pantry, next to which resides a broad step stool able to accommodate a generous girth. *God is on the side of the criminal tonight,* I think. I clap my hands, allowing only the fingers to touch, nearly losing the pocket light in the process of gleefully whispering, "Yes, yes, yes." I move carefully toward the stool and slowly lower my derriere to the top step, from where I am able to shine the light inside the small warren of pans. "Eureka," I whisper as I am confronted by the reflection of light from flimsy metal and cellophane. I take a deep breath and exhale it slowly, for I can hardly believe in this treasure. I have found gold, and it is the mother lode, no less—a veritable bonanza. I have found both Royal Dansk and Oreos. The package of Oreos is stacked neatly on top of the metal Dansk container. *What a snob I used to be. Only the best for me. Now I'll forage at night like a raccoon and eat anything of a compromising nature. You old whore!* I must remain totally alert in opening the Dansk. I carefully lift the Oreo package from the Dansk container and place it on the floor next to the stool. Then, using my left hand as a lever against the lower shelf, I reach inside with my right to slowly lift the Dansk to my lap, troubling over how I will open it. My pocket light has only nail clippers attached. In a pinch, they will be useful in cutting the tape seal. I softly feel around the edges of the metal container resting on my lap. *Oy Gospodi.* I sigh with relief. *Can this be?* The container has been opened already; the tape seal is broken, and the cover has been replaced. *Yes, God is on my side tonight. Hmmm,* I think, *someone has already dispatched a part of the contents.* Nonetheless, I must not become overconfident. I must work slowly and carefully. Suddenly, I hear myself giggle as if I am engaged in robbing a vault of the Hope Diamond. *Be vigilant and listen. If the gorgon hears me, there'll be the devil to pay.* But then I think, *Yob s'ney.* I chuckle at my own irreverence. *If Electra could hear me now! Yob s' toboyu,* I think. I feel exhilarated at my sudden freedom. To curse and to blaspheme is to be. *Hold the container from the outside, lest it topple to the floor while I am removing the cover. Take care that the wrapper does not crackle. Be aware of any alarming sounds, and be prepared to stop even your breathing to prevent discovery. Alas!*

The cookies stare up at me, the ridged ones and the sugar-coated others, like jewels in the night. *Mission nearly accomplished! I shall take only one, a ridged one, and save it for when I am safely tucked away in my bed. Well, let me take another for good measure,* I think. *For tomorrow. I deserve sugar-coated jewels for my trouble.* I tuck them into the pocket of my nightdress. How intoxicating the smell is. But I cannot dwell in this ecstasy of aromas until the task is done and I am back in my own bed. I must concentrate on the mission. *We are not out of the pantry yet. Careful now. Return the lid just as it was. Kharasho.* Now for the Oreos. This package has not been opened yet. *Never mind. No time to be greedy. I'll save Oreos for my next life, if I am reborn as a cockroach.*

Today I'm not diabetic, I think to myself. *Today I am a young girl in braids and a flowered taffeta dress, sitting on a hillside in the shade of a tree in a country that doesn't exist any longer. At least not in the way it did then. Today I am looking at a rainbow and reading into it a radiant future with a boy who is forbidden yet who unequivocally belongs.* I remove the rippled sugar cookie from my pocket and briefly rub it against my cheek, smelling its heaven. *If I eat it now,* I think, *it will leave no telltale crumbs in my sheets. The gorgon will be looking with a loupe. She will say, "Elementary, my dear Watson. The old lady has been eating sugar again. Cause of illness: sugar. Cause of sorrow: granddaughter deprivation and Oreo-devouring daughter-in-law. Cause of death: life."* I am amused and again startled by the sound of my own chortle. I bite into the cookie. I shall die with pleasure.

It is time. I have been waiting forever to compose this letter to Josip, to say all of the things I have never been able to say before. I want to tell him that all of the days of my life, I have remembered the smells and flavors of his body as if we were still children hiding in our secret place just large enough for both of us and two bicycles. "The earth under my face smelled like mushrooms," I will say. "Dark and damp. Remember? We huddled like rabbits, licking sugar and cinnamon from each other's fingers. Our bodies fit together as perfectly as one hand in a glove in a pocket of the earth. I was sure that my happiness was a reward for being obedient all my life. God was granting me this wonder for my diligent service of prayers and genuflection. You were a gift, my reward as I lay with nothing but infinite hope in my heart, surrounded by stones and mildew and bark, facedown in it, inhaling the dank and delicious earth that would prove my ruin. I was delirious then. I am thankful even now."

I want to tell him it wasn't me; no, it wasn't my fault. Josip will understand. "*Dorogoy* Josip. *Prekracniy* Josip. Dear Josip. Lovely Josip." I take another bite of cookie and chew it slowly. It seems to dissolve before I can swallow. "I want to tell you that I never again knew the joy of those moments so long ago, as if life was promising a miracle of unceasingly beautiful days ahead. I was afraid, Josip, but I must confess. When the lieutenant appeared, it was as if out of nowhere. He was not alone. His soldiers had guns and wore helmets that glistened in the sun. He didn't threaten; he smiled. His perfect teeth were like small guillotines. It was me he wanted to interrogate.

'Does Yeva live here?' he asked in his faultless Russian, making no effort to modulate his voice. He spoke our strange tongue flawlessly and smiled his perfect smile, a blue-eyed devil with brilliant white teeth." I pause for another bite of the cookie, effortless pleasure. I lick my lips again.

I lose my train of thought and need to start again. "*Dorogoy Josip.* A person waits a lifetime to know what matters truly in this life. If we could only know it starting out. A new morning with shiny yellow insects, God's expendable toys—like the first glimpse of the rainbow, like that donkey's probing sex. That is what we do. Isn't it, Josip? Probe and hope and experiment, trying each time to get it right and each time making a different mistake. Szymborgska, the Polish poet, writes, 'we come here improvised and leave without the chance to practice.' Lavrentii's Italian colleague once said about economics that on paper it works perfectly as long as you don't inject humans into the equations. Love too is easy without the humans; relations, and a lifetime of living too." I bite into the cookie again. It crumbles in my hand. "*Dorogoy* Josip. You ran when you might have stayed. I, on the other hand, stayed to meet the devil while remembering the promise of God. I, on the other hand, have dreamed worlds around you."

Suddenly, I am tired. I have lost my train of thought again and need to close my eyes for just a moment to catch my breath.

Interlude

I am adrift like a condor hovering on a wind current, my eyesight sharp as gunpowder. I am a bat hanging loosely from the rafters, waiting to swoop. But who am I? I see an old woman drifting toward the edge of an imaginary ocean heaving to reach her, to cradle her in its waves. Her hands and feet are swollen and heavy, her eyelids droop, and the skin of her cheeks is covering the bones of her face like a wet paper napkin.

She is beginning to lose her equilibrium. She sits on the pantry stepladder, forcing her generous derriere onto the second step. From where I'm suspended, I see grand vistas of sweets stacked on the lower shelves, behind pots and pans—hidden. Why should there be anything there? She bends forward just enough to reach the handle of the lowest skillet and then pulls back the stack to see something that startles her even more in this time of dark intrigues. *I am a tough old bird,* she thinks, *but this is more than even I can resist.* She liberates her rump with difficulty from the step stool and, without considering the consequences, kneels to reach more deeply into the shelf to extract its precious store. "Like a chimpanzee. If I am treated like one, then I will act like one," she whispers. She manages a smile at her childish petulance in light of such serious matters. "*Oy Gospodi.*" She hears herself gasping at what is revealed. "I know that smell. The object is soft like bread. Has God sent me a messenger? *Oy Gospodi.* Arnold Cinnamon," she says, reading the name out loud in the dark, though she needs only a sense of smell to understand what she is holding. "Bread. With raisins," she whispers. Like a small child, she has put her finger to her lips to keep any more telltale sounds from escaping. "*Scandal,*" she mutters in her once-native Russian. *Oy Gospodi*, she thinks again. "A fresh, new loaf. If I open the package, she'll know I was here as clearly as if I had written it with indelible pen: 'Eva was here, pilfering the cinnamon raisin bread.' She'll explode, grow horns, and bare fangs." She snickers under her breath, though her heart is racing. She knows she is being mischievous. Tomorrow morning, when Mercy arrives, she'll tell her what she has done. "I'll only tell her about the cinnamon bread in case her mother has sworn her to a pact to protect Grandma from herself. I shall eat only one slice from the middle of the loaf. No one will notice."

The operation is to pull the green plastic clip from the outside packaging. No mean feat for her gnarled fingers, she simply tears it—with constrained capabilities, rather violently—from its hold on the neck of the package. She allows herself this one carelessness.

There is more packaging inside, the kind with crinkly paper, which must be penetrated with quiet precision. This she does slowly with minimum noise. The flap comes away easily. She pulls out several slices from the end; takes an inside piece; places it gently into her lap; returns what is left in her hand; closes the package as well as can be expected; grabs around for the outside wrapper, which, thankfully, is within easy reach; and returns the slightly diminished single-wrap loaf to its original plastic. *Double-unwrap-and-wrap operation complete,* she thinks, but then she remembers the little green clip, which has fallen under the shelf far too deeply for her to retrieve. Her knees are beginning to throb. *You win some, and you lose some. Good enough, Sherlock.* She must return the loaf to where she found it. She turns the loaf around, placing the open end toward the inside of the lower shelf. Gasping for air, she lifts herself carefully and reinserts her aged derriere back onto the second rung of the stepstool. She thinks of the Pink Panther and is amused at her comic guile. She is stealing bread like the Aesopian crow. *Rest now,* she tells herself, though her fingers are trembling and her seventy-seven-year-old heart pounds like an advancing cannon. Aloud, she says, "If I die now, I can do no better. *Uspokoysya*, Eva. Calm yourself. You are not a criminal." She tears a small piece of bread off and raises it gently to her nose, breathing through the bread, in and then out evenly, as if the slice carries the properties of oxygen to a suffocating lung. It has the effect of hallucinatory incense, her magic mushroom, her church. She wishes to be frozen this way for eternity, with a piece of sweetness at her lips. If only Lavinia could see her now. She cackles again quietly. When she bites into the bread, it makes her feel as she did more than sixty years ago, when she was a young girl who had never tasted cinnamon or pomegranates and lived in a village without running water—she had a well. She might have ended up there with a nice Russian or Ukrainian boy who drank for pleasure or pain or power. Is it possible that a combination of flour, sugar, cinnamon, and eggs can taste like heaven to this doomed mortal?

"Ambrosia," she says. "Cinnamon bread, the food of gods and kings. Forget fish or meat or vegetables."

Energized and enlivened, she begins her letter again: "*Dorogoy* Josip. The lieutenant smiled, and his Russian was perfect. He didn't threaten, because he didn't need to. '*Gde nakhoditsa eto mesto?*' He put his face close to mine. He smelled freshly shaven and showered, like the master race he was sent to the hinterland to represent. We peasants were in the presence of a god who spoke better Russian than we did. 'Where is this place?' he asked again. 'Where are they hiding?' I could smell the soap on his skin, the sweetness of his healthy breath. I knew he had eaten oats. *Haferflocken*. We called them *Hafye Flyokie* in the DP camps. But that was later, when we forced our children to eat whether they wanted to or not, because food was plentiful, and food—any food—was good and could save them. Dear Josip. It was *our* hiding place, Josip—yours and mine. The officer's smiling blue eyes were like needles, and when he pointed them in my direction, I thought my quaking legs would not support me. You were gone by then, and I was afraid."

Her head hangs. The half-eaten slice of bread has fallen to the floor. With effort, she reaches to pick it up. It is wet with her tears and soiled with beach sand not yet swept up in yesterday's cleaning. She takes another bite. She does not notice how ordinary sand sweetened by sugar and cinnamon crunches under her decomposing gums.

When she opens her eyes again, she does not comprehend how she has landed on the floor. She is sitting on one leg, facing the step stool. As she tries to lift her body from the contortion in which it finds itself, her leg is beset by thousands of tiny, piercing needles with their own mind for cruelty, and she understands—and feels— that her foot is dangerously asleep. Her presence of mind is quickly deserting but remains enough to caution her; she dare not scream for help. She frantically wonders how she will ever raise herself from this position and transport herself back to the safety of her bed. The loaf of cinnamon raisin bread resting on her lap is open at both ends. There are crumbs all over her nightgown and bits of mauled bread strewn around her body like a magician's ring of destiny. "*Oy Gospodi*" is all she can sputter. Somewhere in the deeper recesses of her brain, she silently laments the ridiculousness of her current state and bewails the stupidity of a stubborn old woman, a once-war-torn refugee who has seen and felt the proverbial horrors, now surrounded by incriminating shreds of commercially baked products of a mundane variety. She remains seated with her foot relentlessly pricked by the needles, which, refusing to let up, intensify their incessant jabbing, while steadfastly telling herself she must regain her strength for the journey back to her room, to her bed, to safety. Her arms and legs have become weights. If only her foot would wake up. She needs to rest her head for a moment. But when she closes her eyes and tries to lay her head softly on the top rung of the step stool, her shoulders fold inward abruptly, she loses control, and on the spot where her backside found refuge, her head lands with a comical thud, although by this time, she hardly notices.

Forgiveness

It's hard to live, but sometimes it is harder to die.

Before Mercy disappeared, she asked me where memories go when we die. "I'm a member of the ignorant and blithering elderly club," I told her, "not Carl Sagan. He knows. Somewhere on the other side, he knows." Poor Mercy. I left her wondering out loud who Carl Sagan was and myself realizing the unbridgeable breach between our stories, except in print. Mine has just about expired, and hers is yet to be written. Should I be comforted that she will soon embark upon her own journey, forgetting about her adoring grandmother and loving, hating, and then loving again those persons who love her most? It is no secret that struggles define us, though many of those struggles remain secret even from ourselves, protected by the stupid yet persistent anomalies of thought and behavior, as if we are built inside out or upside down, obsessed with reversals of desire and repugnance, advance and retreat. It is a simple thing, really, explained over and over again each time we crawl into the sunlight: we want what we cannot have and reject what is ours for the asking. Perhaps memories are converted into energy before being swallowed by the earth. Perhaps they infiltrate human dreams and spread like knowledge over vast populations—armies of diluted intelligence, clustering sometimes into meaningful thoughts, pulsing nodes of electricity going on and off in a dark universe like tiny insignificant fragments of light. They are bouncing, falling, sometimes devouring in agony, and other times enveloping in warmth these tiny creatures that inhabit this world. *Ping. Ping. Pong.*

I'll tell that to Mercy tomorrow when she comes.

Letters from a Friend

Lavrentii Jr.

When we found Eva that morning, we realized the worst had happened. Working together, Lavinia and I managed to lift her head from the stool and straighten her contorted body to the floor. Lavinia insisted we not move her any more than was necessary. We succeeded in cleaning, more or less, the mess of bread and cookie crumbs she had left. I swept around her while Lavinia washed away the dried blood that had accumulated over her left eye. There was a gash, which Lavinia carefully cleansed. When the ambulance arrived, Mother looked freshly washed, although she had, by this time, already slipped into a coma. Lavinia, ever the faithful physician, oversaw Mother's transfer to the stretcher and removal to the hospital. She rode with her while I followed behind in the car. Thankfully, Mercy was not there to witness these events.

When Lavinia wanted to spare Mercy even the visits to the hospital, I had to put my foot down, and this time, I prevailed. I felt that the pain of not having said good-bye to her grandmother would have greater consequences than not seeing her at all. We all need closure. I also felt Lavinia was trying too hard to protect Mercy from life. In no uncertain terms, I told her, she should not imagine her own life as a blueprint for Mercy's. She will just need to trust the child's instincts. I believe Mercy was a comforting presence to the old woman, even in her state of sleep. She held Eva's hand, and at moments, I could swear Eva was listening. Mercy said Eva smiled when she told her about the Glass Museum, and when she mentioned Josip, she seemed a bit agitated. Mercy noticed her eyes moving and the closed eyelids fluttering. When I gently pressed Mercy for more information on Josip, her eyes teared up, and she placed her cheek on Eva's hand. But she didn't say a word, and I knew better than to insist. Even Lavinia knew enough to let it go.

Eva lasted this way for about a week.

The difference between a wife and a mother—one of the differences, that is—is that your mother is always your mother. The tyranny of biology makes servants of us all. You could argue it's all in your head. You could argue it's all in your genes and your cells. You could argue that connections of a scientific nature have meaning beyond the visible. Is this just mumbo-jumbo or a way of believing in God?

I was the one—yes, it was me—who had suggested to Mercy that she stay with Maribel for a couple of nights. Mother and Grandmother needed a bit of time to sort things out, I told her. Living together for these past few days had created frictions. Perhaps this was a bad idea. If Mother had been the kind of person who would tell you openly what she really wanted, if she had been easier to read, she would have been easier to deal with. Instead, it was always a guessing game, trying to decipher her real feelings. She could smile and despise at the same time. I saw it often when I was a child, and we were regular churchgoers. She could be polite, even flattering, to the blowhards who often tried to catch and hold her attention with stories suggesting their heroism or cleverness. "*Boltun.* Gas bag," she would mutter under her breath to me or Branka while holding her smile. On the other hand, she also had a dog's loyalty in her. She never abandoned Branka for the academic glitterati surrounding my father, and she never sought out their company or favored it over Branka's. Branka might have been simple in her direct goodness, but she was never unaware. Branka's friendship was the only connection she retained, as far as I could see, to a life she had once known and abandoned in Ukraine. I had never heard a word about this Josip from her. Honestly, when Mercy brought it up at the dinner table, I assumed Eva had just been telling her more stories, embellishing her adventures because she knew that it was an entertainment for Mercy.

When my father was alive, my mother suffered terrible nightmares. I used to hear them from where I slept. She screamed in an inarticulate voice that undulated from deep within her body. Dare I say *soul*? I once heard her begging for forgiveness: "Oh God, forgive me. Forgive me."

"You were just a child," my father used to say to console her. "Just a child."

When I asked her what kind of nightmares she had, what she heard, and whom she talked to, she just laughed it off and told me she was running from the bogeyman. "You could hear me?" she asked. "I'll try to keep the volume down next time." And there were many next times. She was regular with her nightmares, like a geyser.

* * *

When we cleaned out her house, the house I had grown up in, we found a picture and letters she had saved. The letters were interesting but did little to explain this woman, who was, admittedly, peculiar. There was a letter from her father, telling her that her brother had died after being executed by the Germans, and there were some love letters from my father scattered in a box in no particular order. Order was not her thing. She didn't like to accumulate things, so it was telling for us that these few mementos must have been deeply significant for her.

If I have learned nothing else from my mother, I have learned this: the description of a life is not ever a simple chronology of events; its deeper meanings often hide in the folds and crevasses of expression and linger in its silences. One of these silences had to do with a man named Josip. As I have said, my mother was neither acquisitive nor orderly with her mementos, with one notable exception. Josip's few letters were found carefully stored in a manila envelope in the top drawer of her bedside dresser, along with several pens and a few pictures that never made it to the mantel. The envelope clasp was broken, and the top fold was partially torn. The letters themselves were held together with a rubber band, and they were arranged in chronological order, a couple with small sticky notes affixed. Nothing was written on the notes. They seemed to serve as bookmarks for other thoughts or references that only she carried around in her head. At least that is how I understood them. One of the small photographs in the drawer, a picture with uneven, corrugated edges, which I remember having seen as a child, shows Eva as a young girl with braids and a pretty flowered dress. She is wearing white socks and dark, flat shoes. She is walking arm in arm with a similarly dressed young woman who, Mother once told me, is Branka. She and Branka are hardly recognizable. They are smiling into the lens. It is remarkable that these two sylphs could not then have guessed how far afield their lives would tumble.

On the lower shelf of this bedside dresser, we found the bedspread I had brought back from Mirgorod, the one given to me by her long-since-dead father. It was protected in moth balls and neatly wrapped in plastic. I had nearly forgotten about it. When I gave it to her, she took it away, and I did not see it again until now.

These letters were written by someone who signed his name as Иосип, which is the English equivalent of Joseph. They were hard to translate because the Russian was corrupted by English words, and there was virtually no punctuation. It was as if the writer's Russian had been arrested at a certain age and any new words had come from another language source. I have tried to give the thoughts and ideas contained in them some cohesion and clarity, though more than once, I have had to guess. Fortunately—or perhaps unfortunately—for my mother, there were few of these to transcribe.

* * *

Haifa
March 17, 1966
Dear Eva,

It was wonderful and quite a surprise to see you again. You were, of course, older, but your face hadn't really changed, and the expression you carried—you were looking at something on the ground—reminded me of the way you looked when you tasted some of the fruits at my father's stand. I knew even from far away that it was you. What a miracle. How many years now? Thirty? More? I still ask myself how it is possible.

You ask how we came to be here. Stories behind the stories we are told, as if there exists a whole other world of being. Not like ghosts—or maybe yes, like ghosts—we carry with us. They describe those we have lost, and through them, we manage to preserve their connection to us, though we stop speaking of them. I lost my mother during the war, but my father I found again when it was all over. So you will forgive me if I am not able to tell you more about our eventual departure from Mirgorod and from Europe. Much you have already learned from your newspapers and history books, and the details are here unimportant, at least for our lost-and-found friendship, and I suspect you know too much already.

My wife is a good woman, and she has given me two children who exasperate me and fill me with the greatest pride and happiness. Sometimes I wonder how I have come to deserve this happiness after everything else. I have loved being a father but only now can understand that it is not easy bringing children into this world. Although we live a comfortable life, there is always a danger of more war and more death. Even today, especially today.

I have told you about my Shimon, who is now in the army. He was never a particularly good student, so perhaps the militaries will teach him some discipline. He was always his mother's favorite. Eva continues her studies and makes me prouder every day.

Otherwise, life goes on as ever—slowly from the inside and so quickly from without.

I may need to visit the United States again soon. I will let you know when this might come about.

And how is your little wonder boy?

* * *

Haifa
April 22, 1967
Dear Eva,

Thank you for your letters.

Forgive my long absence. I have thought about you often.

It is wonderful that your son is doing so well. He will probably follow in his father's footsteps and become a professor. You should be very proud of him. I am sorry I had no chance to meet him when I was last in New York. I am truly glad you have found such a good man and made such a strong family. In the turbulence of this world, it's all we can depend on, yes?

We have had a minor crisis. My wife has been sick, but with God's help, she will recover. My Shimon continues to serve in the army. He has become a disciplined soldier and recently attained the rank of first lieutenant. On one hand, this is good, because he has finally been able to distinguish himself—I told you he was a very regrettable student, although he was smart enough. On the other hand, I am afraid he will always be part of the military. Perhaps involvement with militaries will always be our destiny, to wait for the next assault. Eva is nearly done with her medical studies. She has even talked about doing research in the United States. Perhaps she will visit you someday, but I don't think it will happen, since she seems to be in love with a nice medical student, who also is a military boy.

On balance, my business runs well. I have been traveling recently in Kiev. It is never easy having dealings with those *khokhli*—you will forgive me the use of this word, which my mother often used—and it is not easy for me to return there for any reasons. But I do what I must. I have worked hard for what I have, and it is all I know. We are not wealthy, but we have enough to live comfortably. What more can a person ask?

Several months ago, I met someone who was born in Mirgorod. It made me think of how we were then, especially you. Always the strong one, the daring girl. It all might have been different without a war. A candle that is left to burn itself out is more easily forgotten than the one that burns your fingertips as you are extinguishing it. You will see that unlike you, I am no poet, no Pushkin.

My best wishes.

* * *

Haifa
November 23, 1968
Dear Eva,

When Shimon went to war, I thought my heart would break. Though I have given up praying long ago, I prayed. But we were lucky. He came back a more serious man, not so easy with a smile as before. War, fighting, death makes you so. This is nothing new to you. Eva was also involved in the hospitals. Such trials for a young doctor. But this is life. She is finding meaning in her work. I ask when she will marry her medical military boy. When all the fighting is over, she says. That might be a long time.

We are well. Thank you for asking. And your wonder boy?

* * *

Haifa

January 1971

Dear Eva,

I am afraid the time has gotten away from me. My wife was sick again, and we have been caring for her. Eva is here often. It is important to have a doctor in the family who can translate the language of the medical persons. They are too busy to explain the complications and possibilities of disease. Unfortunately, we must depend too heavily on my daughter, who cannot find it easy to continue practicing and training while she is awaiting her first child. Yes, she married, but a completely different boy. From one day to the next, she told us her military medical boy was out of the picture. She had found her dream, a young Ethiopian physicist—a rare occurrence, I think. But I am happy for her and actually look forward to a little brown grandchild. Shimon is still Shimon and still in the military. He is very important today.

You ask me many questions about our last days in Mirgorod, but I am not able to say much more. I remember and forget because it was so long ago, and we were so young. But there are moments that will stay with me forever, because I learned to be a man with you, to take my responsibilities seriously. Nothing is easy. We must try.

Your Josip

* * *

There are several other letters with pages missing, abrupt endings, or indecipherable script, making it impossible to assemble a coherent whole. Even the dates, when they are not altogether absent from the page, seem implausible. In those, I sensed reluctance on Josip's part to continue writing. The letters became shorter and more perfunctory until they stopped in December 1972, in which Josip wrote that his daughter gave birth to a girl whom they named after her grandmother.

Joseph is someone Mother knew in Ukraine before the war. I could not ascertain any special relationship from these letters, though they must have known each other well to have struck up this correspondence after thirty years. He speaks of Mirgorod, the city where she was born and lived until, as a young girl, she was transported to the German Reich to work as a laborer in a munitions factory. Unlike Branka, who returned several times to Ukraine after restrictions were lifted and travel throughout the region became easier, my mother never returned and never saw her family again. She did continue to write to her parents intermittently, and I believe Branka became her emissary to this, her forbidden world. Only her parents were left. Her brother had died in the war, and her father was to die later. In fact, in one of her few revelations to me—actually, she mentioned it at the dinner table; my father was alive then—she revealed that she had received a letter through Branka from someone in her village, informing her of her father's death. She also told us she had seen in her dreams her house or a similar house with dark, heavy smoke billowing from the chimney the night before she got the news, as if she wanted us to believe that she had foreseen it. This was long after she had left the church and begun despising its holiness. That is all I ever knew about her life there. With the newly found letters from Josip, the portrait is as complete as it will ever be. One might say our Eva has died undiscovered. One might say she has given us more than we have a right to know.

I briefly thought about sending a note to the address on the envelopes from Josip, informing the recipient of Eva's death, but decided against it. Too much time had gone by. We buried her with a picture Lavinia had once taken of a younger Mercy and Eva laughing together at the dinner table from the days not so long ago, when Eva was still the master of her household, along with all of the letters, which Mercy placed lovingly alongside the casket. We laid her mother's bedspread over her feet. Finally, we laid her beloved Bazarov under her hands, which were folded in the shape of a cross over her heart.

Intruder

Sarah had long ago given up living on the outside. She smiled but didn't participate; she spoke when certain things needed to be said; and she lied in order to more easily evade obstacles in common discourse—without malice but, rather, with convenience in mind.

If someone asked, "How are you?" the answer was always "Fine"—no more and no less. No one cared deeply. Of this she was certain. Why bore strangers with details?

"How's William doing?"

"Fine. Thank you. Enjoying himself."

The door was locked. Few were allowed to enter.

The world in her head, on the other hand, was much kinder, more interesting, and better controlled. There, the events of daily experience played themselves out like the strings of an orchestra. Great intervals of time were steeped in melancholy memories of a past that had never happened. Verbal battles were fought, psychological wars were conveniently won, and great loves were found and wasted. The days of her life turned like the pages of a book, passing like the events in a novel. By living the introspective life, she had the advantage of being able to rewrite the chapters, trying on various endings for fit, all the while accepting the notion that life was strange, love was tragic, and outcomes were unpredictable. Dialogue was pithy and to the point. No words were wasted in the interchange between opposing sides.

* * *

When Manolo came to stay with them to study English, it was understood to be for a couple of months. When they picked him up at the airport in a rainstorm in early October, their son, Zachary, was not with them. Zach was a senior at a small college in neighboring Vermont and had been unable to come down during a weekday. Classes were in session, and he had an important exam, so he said he would call later.

The plane had been unable to taxi to the gate, so departing passengers had to run to escape the driving rain. It was William, extending his hand, who spoke first. "*Hola*, Manolo. *Cómo estás?*"

Manolo, looking wet and proud, returned the gesture with a slight tip of his head. "Thank you very much." It was clear at the outset that he was a young man with a purpose. Not then and not later did he resort to Spanish to make his wishes clear, although he knew that both William and Sarah would understand him. It would be English always, he insisted tacitly, and his resolve never wavered.

"Where is Zach?"

Looking around, he seemed slightly discombobulated by the noticeable absence of his friend. William's explanation reassured him. Doing a swift recovery, he brandished his politeness as if to protect himself from the unknown. "Thank you very much," he repeated with a barely noticeable nod of his head.

* * *

Zachary and Manolo had met while the former was taking his junior year in Barcelona. William and Sarah had consented because Zachary had asked. "It'll be a great opportunity. I'll be back before you know it. My Spanish will improve." Zach was a student of Latin American cultures, but for reasons he'd never made clear to his parents, he'd chosen to pursue a wonderful opportunity to study the mutual histories of the Hispanic lands in Spain. It made sense. Spain had started it all.

William had countered, "But they don't speak Castilian in Barcelona." The logic of studying in a region where the local population defied convention to speak their local tongue escaped William's understanding.

"They don't speak *only* Castilian. I'll come back knowing Catalan as well."

And so it had happened. It had been a wonderful year for Zach. He had written long and detailed e-mails about his experiences at the university, the foods he had discovered, and the friends he had made. Sarah, with her feminine intuition, had suspected he had fallen in love· for the first time, although Zach was careful never to allude to a particular woman. Whether this supposition was based on fact or was a product of Sarah's rich inner universe mattered less than its real possibility. They had encountered a milestone, real or imagined, in their collective lives, and one way or another, they knew that things would be different.

William and Sarah could also remember several references to Manolo, including one in connection with a running bull and another regarding women and wine. Based on the strength of this friendship, evidently, Manolo felt he could stay with Zach's family while doing something constructive and useful. His thesis—something about environmental studies—required the reading of source materials in English. William and Sarah had agreed that for him, studying English was like killing two birds with one stone: he could proceed in his pursuit of his academic goal and, at the same time, avoid, at least for a short time, the responsibilities bearing down upon him.

* * *

"He's a great guy—won't bother you. He's quiet and has a lot of charisma," Zach had said. They had wondered at first what quiet and charisma had to do with each other, believing Zach had meant he had charm instead. Despite the kind of reservations hosts might harbor for a guest with an open-ended return ticket, they accepted his presence philosophically. He was their son's friend and their honored guest. They would treat him with the utmost courtesy. Privately, they wished him success but hoped his sojourn would end swiftly. They had become accustomed to the kind of tranquility that sets in when beloved children were fulfilling promise, staying safe, and, above all, living elsewhere.

* * *

"Mark my words," William had said. "He'll want to stay the year."

"We'll just tell him he can't. That's all," Sarah had answered, unwilling to engage in speculation about Manolo's long-term intentions. Sarah had other lives to visit and no time for details. In her mind, his insignificant satellite would orbit around their planets, always seen but never understood—quiet, withdrawn, bright on some days, and invisible on others. It would be slightly able to affect the tides, take its brilliance from an outside source, and be uninteresting, really, to the heavenly bodies holding the satellite in place. Sarah didn't actually think these things; this was the way the universe was constructed in her mind. On the other hand, she was not without feeling. Stray puppies, lost souls, and wandering parasites gravitated in her direction with magnetic force. Such creatures found her soothing because she treated them no differently than she treated the members of her family, at least temporarily. As long as they made no demands on her emotionally, she accepted them and gave them shelter. Some thought her frigid. Otherwise, she was exceptionally well protected, which, more often than not, was a byproduct of fear and trembling. She simply preferred her solitude.

* * *

Zachary was the unexpected child of love, youth, and hope. He was always a surprise, and he did everything without warning. He was like a warm and refreshing raindrop during a hot spell, a glimmer of light in a dark tunnel, a spark of unexpected energy during the doldrums. He was born a month early at the end of a lively dinner. Contusion and fracture were common as he grew. He fell from rocks, collided with trees, and, on one occasion, was blindsided by a car that cracked his shin. He skied often where it was forbidden and over moguls or through densely wooded areas, jumping, crashing, and bruising as he went along. Undaunted, he ran with Spanish bulls, coming recklessly close to those tortured and frightfully dangerous creatures. And he always did so with a smile, because like most young men his age, he believed himself invincible and immortal.

"Isn't Pamplona the city where they run with bulls in the street?" she had asked William after receiving a postcard with a Pamplona postmark. The face of the card showed a picture of a bright yellow paella and a smiling Spanish senorita in full local regalia.

"Yes, darling."

At times, she would imagine Zach engaged in a lusty flamenco with a gorgeous raven-haired gypsy flinging her gold earrings with each clap of the castanets. She loved being an imaginary participant in her son's life. She might watch from a remote table in a café without danger of being recognized. In her daydreams, he always made the right decisions, never compromising safety for love, money, or adventure. The little vignettes amused and gratified her and served to comfort her in the illusion that she could govern the outcome of events. It was a game she played for the sake of her own survival, for she somehow sensed that her golden child was a bit of a daredevil.

Perhaps his behavior was an extension of what Sarah had noticed as a not-so-secret desire to test the limits of danger. When he was a small child of five, she observed him trying to insert a fork into an electrical socket—after being told it could cause shock and even death. But how much did a child of five understand? When he was thrown halfway across the living room and landed in an apparently lifeless heap, Sarah was struck dumb and useless. Paralyzed, she was unable even to cry for help. It was fortunate that William was home at the time and that they lived next door to the veterans' hospital. William picked up the limp child and ran like the current to the emergency room. Sarah did not remember much from the events of that day, and she deliberately knew even less of what the doctors did to bring him back to life. When Zach walked out of the emergency room, he was holding the doctor's hand and licking an ice-cream cone. When she saw him, Sarah's limbs began to tremble, and her body began to vibrate as if it were the epicenter of a seismic episode. In one blow, the entire precariousness of existence and happiness came crashing down upon her. Shortly after this incident, she began having nightmares, like a geyser that must regularly release. Once, she dreamed in black and white of holding Zach back from the clutches of an angry ravine. On another occasion, she attempted to protect him from being engulfed by fire. William was always there to rescue her and Zach from a dream life whose denouement did not guarantee a happy ending. "It's just a dream, Sarah," he would mumble before turning to sleep again. In Sarah's case, these nightmares brought no relief but were the signs of a continuously bubbling cauldron upon which a cast iron cover had been securely placed. Although it was Zach's near miss, it was her lesson, learned deeply and held tightly within.

* * *

Zach seemed always to be short of money. Although he worked hard, he spent faster and was just as likely to borrow as to lend. Money was a commodity to be shared equally among friends. William and Sarah provided him with a monthly allowance. How he used it was his concern. If it wasn't enough, he would simply ask for more.

If they honored his request, he would be spared the necessity of contingency procedures.

Zach was lean and long. Sarah had always wondered whose genes had contributed to his red hair and his translucent skin tainted slightly by the acne around his chin. His deeply set eyes and thick brows gave the impression that he was looking out from within a dark and bottomless cave. They looked secretive and perhaps even dangerous when he wasn't smiling.

Sarah could only speculate on the reasons that made Zach and Manolo friends. They were as different as night and day. The other, she had observed, was cautious, circumspect, thrifty, sluggish, subordinate, and shrewd. He had what was once defined as a cold-weather body: short with powerful legs. Although thin, he tended toward a stockiness that would probably manifest itself in middle age. His skin was olive, and his complexion was smooth.

* * *

When Zach came home and they went out together with his friends, Manolo blended well and adjusted easily. Partially from Zach's efforts, Manolo was protected, and the friendship was sincere. Sarah never learned how the two boys had become friends in Barcelona. Any incursion into their history would have been treated, she was sure, as the meddling of an overprotective parent.

For William, it was all the same. He didn't mind Manolo's presence as long as he remained more or less invisible. Even when he did not, William hardly ever showed his irritation. For one thing, William could more easily block out the world. He read the newspapers and watched TV. For another, he was simply less emotional and more civilized. Sarah, on the other hand, was easily distracted. She hated clutter. For peace, she required emptiness and order—spare furnishings and no useless bric-a-brac. She preferred space unencumbered by objects. The first time she found Manolo's socks left carelessly in the living room, she appeared perplexed. "Manolo, please," she entreated. "For God's sake," she pleaded when he forgot to collect his dirty underwear after a shower. She was annoyed at the buxom creatures painted on his shorts and suffered a mild revulsion at what she deemed his youthful vulgarity. His style more than his substance exasperated her easily. Soon a pattern was established. If it wasn't one thing, it was another. They were small vexations but they were constant. For Sarah, Manolo's presence began to obtrude.

* * *

Manolo spent time learning English at a local school. He was easy with women, probably because he didn't really care about them. They often called the house, leaving messages in heavily accented English or in Spanish that was easy for Sarah to understand. There were more than two who seemed to call with certain regularity. "I miss you" or "Why don't you call me? This is Beatriz. I love you very much" was spoken with a high-pitched yet soft voice whose timbre gave Sarah the impression of neediness, a voice whose possessor begged attention and could soon become tiring. *How easily these women throw around words such as "I love you" and "I miss you,"* she thought. *Where does he find these girls?* She answered her own question. *Probably the daughters of very wealthy South American ranchers who marry early out of convenience or without serious thought, then desert their timid and aging wives for younger women, and then ride off into the sunset to build new haciendas for their newly blushing brides. He must resonate with these girls,* she speculated. She always continued in this vein, for she could not understand how anyone could find him interesting or attractive. These thoughts, as those of an overactive imagination and inherently suspicious nature, she did not share with anyone.

William suspected the source of her irritation but was too busy with newspapers and TV to bother. He had always considered her odd and eccentric. "Yes, darling," he would humor her whenever she became excited about her books, movies, or imagined intrigues between neighbors. He was certain he understood her better than she understood herself—that is, when he took the time to think about such things. William, like homo faber, was a man of science and statistics. He loved his wife because she brought something childlike and unexpected to his life. He knew she needed protection.

* * *

It was decided that while Zach was away at college, Manolo would use his room. Sarah made space in Zach's dresser for Manolo's clothing by clearing the two lower drawers for his things. At first, having Manolo around was no inconvenience. The fact that he slept until early afternoon on the weekends did not bother her. It was clear he needed the time to catch up on rest and slumber. He was a growing boy. During the week, he rose early to arrive at whatever school he was attending. He often left a few minutes before she did and was always careful to avoid any conflict of need where the bathroom was concerned. Despite the size of the house, Sarah and Manolo found themselves in competition for the same shower. The one on Manolo's floor did not work as well. A leak in the stall caused problems on the ceiling of the floor below, and until it was repaired, he was asked to share with the others. (William, not one to lose sight of insignificant annoyances, had been preoccupied of late with more-pressing matters at the lab. He did eventually attend to the problem.) In the meantime, Manolo listened and always asked if she were done using the bathroom before entering for his shower. He was as diffident as a guest was expected to be. By that time, Sarah was usually ready to put on some lipstick and a bit of discreet eye makeup, which she did in her bedroom before leaving.

* * *

Sarah insisted on looking natural. Although she was growing older by the day, she did not color her hair or paint her nails. *Better to look old than unnatural,* she thought. Her one major concession to appearance was a dark, precise line she applied to her lips in hopes of allaying the beasts of time. Well-defined lips gave the illusion of looking younger, she thought—applied magic, an illusionist's trick for the masses. The trick deflected attention away from lines and pouches. In any case, it seemed to work if the reaction of the morning-paper person was any indication. The middle-aged, sun-tanned paperboy (should she call him a man?) continued to make lewd gestures with his lips when she emerged from the subway every morning. Although she pretended not to notice, she was secretly somewhat flattered. Satisfied she could still turn heads with her appearance, she soon became tired of the subterfuge and sought another exit, even though it was inconvenient. How sad, she thought, that a rich life could be punctuated by such trivial vanities.

* * *

Every morning when he ran for the bus, Manolo would call out in his clipped and hurried Castilian accent, "Good-bye, Suhruh!" When he spoke at the dinner table, his speech was softened by the influences of Valencian dialect. He had studied in Barcelona, but he was a native of Valencia, whose idiom was a close relative of Catalan's. When Manolo spoke with relatives in Spain, Sarah and William learned to recognize the bouncing, fluid diphthongs they normally associated with French or Portuguese. *"Com esteu? Que dius? Que feu?"* were phrases often heard in conversations with his mother. But in the mornings, he was official, studied, stark, and public. "Good morrrning. How arrre you?" Especially when he was in a hurry.

One morning, as Sarah prepared to return his salutation, she noticed he was wearing what seemed to be Zach's canvas fisherman's hat. She made no mention of it. Why should she? He was living in

Zach's room; he might as well make use of the clothing Zach had left behind. Zach probably did not want it anyway. As Zach's friend, Manolo was inclined to think he could take liberties with his good friend's apparel. Even when it appeared he was availing himself of more than hats, including trousers, shirts, and belts, she did not allow such incursions to upset her. After all, he was a guest and, as such, would be accorded complete hospitality.

* * *

At the end of the first month, Sarah began secretly to welcome the end of his visit. She wished to return to her routine and to take comfort in private movies she watched through her mind's eye, through which she could continue working, making occasional dinners, and responding robotically to questions put to her by the outside world. She was a master at conducting coherent conversations about matters having little to no relevance for her, as if she were programmed for dual mode: an interactive screen saver with the critical application running in the background, invisible to the viewer. She was a study in sweetness: insipid, innocuous, safe. The boy's presence seemed to upset her equanimity, putting her on alert and disrupting the soft, comfortable, life-saving escape buffer she had painstakingly constructed around herself.

"Do you mind turning down the TV?" she asked Manolo upon returning from work one day and finding him doing homework in the kitchen. "Or go into the TV room and turn down the sound, please." This was her time: the hour before William returned, when she could dream lives uninterrupted and conduct dialogues with imaginary beings from novels that ended badly.

"Sorry." He was accommodating.

"Thank you." But she could still hear Oprah in the background. She was giving tips on losing weight again. *Damn the overweight and pimpled.* She began slamming the plates on the table and chopping hard.

"Manolo, it's still too loud." She knew he wasn't listening. His excuse for surround sound, total immersion, was learning by osmosis.

"What's the use?" she lamented under her breath. "By the time Oprah is over, William will be home, and I'll be bludgeoned with the news of the world. At least Manolo's days are numbered." This consoling thought enabled a short, successful drift into a fictional ménage à trois in which the betrayed general of the novel, ennobled by grief and patience, confronted his betrayer to seek understanding. She thought about the Hungarian author, who had died in obscurity. "A suicide after eighty-nine years. I wonder if he felt more betrayed than betrayer. Why did he wait so long to die?" For Sarah, such daytime interludes were like preludes to sleep. They were harder now because of Oprah but not impossible. But unlike those who lulled themselves with questions about the nature of the stars and planets, Sarah dived into alternate characters as if she were practicing for any eventuality that her humdrum life could deliver. She always performed better inside than when confronted with the real thing.

* * *

In December, Manolo asked William if, in January, he could return for another couple of months. He said, "If I go back to Spain now, I will lose everything I have learned." When William consented, somewhat grudgingly, Sarah did not say a word. She felt that if she had survived the first couple of months, she could overcome the next. But she secretly entertained the hope that he would change his mind, his parents might protest—after all, so much time could be an imposition, or he'd find a new girlfriend in Spain or need to be rid of the last one here in Brookline. Perhaps he would win the lottery, or some misfortune—not serious, of course—would sabotage his plans to finish English. Thus, he would be forced to undertake the arduous and boring task of completing his thesis.

When he returned in January, however, it was as if, again, he had fallen out of the sky.

* * *

On the morning she saw him with Zach's new white tennis sneakers, she recoiled slightly. She said nothing, choosing instead to examine her own irritation. Why couldn't she just be a better person than she was? Was she so selfish? A misanthrope at heart? Mean-spirited and measuring? Did she stay awake nights, worrying she might have done too much for the boy? Why was she always alert in his presence, always noticing and always anticipating without asking? Did she expect others to be able to read her mind? Why should it disturb her that the young man in Zachary's room was making himself at home, adapting comfortably to his surroundings? Did she expect him to continue to keep a safe distance and be timid and deferential at all times?

Some habits she legitimately disliked, and she had no trouble telling him so, firmly and unequivocally. When he left his tray with a dirty plate and glass in the middle of the living-room floor and went off to study, she called him on it immediately. Did he expect a maid to pick up after him? Was this a hotel? He agreed without contrition that his behavior was an unacceptable oversight, and it never happened again. In fact, he became careful to clean up after himself, to put away plates and cutlery and load and unload the dishwasher. In this respect, he played the part of a conscientious albeit long-staying guest.

But the matter of the clothes seemed to discombobulate her more. Was it because the clothing belonged to Zach and he hadn't been asked? It seemed Manolo was quietly making forays into forbidden minefields where the perception and reality of separating lines had no clear definition.

* * *

When Zach failed to return on Monday night to university housing, neither William nor Sarah was overly concerned. Both assumed there was a reasonable explanation—William because he was a rational man for whom scientific probabilities governed the nature of events, and Sarah because the alternative to a reasonable explanation was unthinkable. Zach and a classmate had decided to drive over the Canadian border for some serious skiing. It was a long weekend after a grueling period of midterm exams. Manolo had remained behind for reasons unclear to Sarah—because of a woman perhaps. On Tuesday, they received a call from a housemate wondering why the two young men had not returned.

If, on that Tuesday night, Sarah could have turned herself inside out, she would have. Prevented by an unnamable thread, an invisible compulsion, she continued to wash lettuce and chop onions for the salad as if naught were amiss. Manolo returned later than usual from school and asked if she needed any help making the dinner. She politely accepted his offer of assistance.

"Why, thank you." She noticed for the first time that he had an earring just like Zach's.

"May I get some crockery for you?" He looked at his feet while he spoke.

She smiled. "We don't usually use that word in American English. *Plates* is fine. Yes."

"And cutlery?" He was suddenly emboldened by her friendliness.

"We don't want to give your mother reason for concern. I don't think you have been eating well lately." How young he appeared suddenly. He was just a boy like her own.

He set the table while she boiled pasta and heated spaghetti sauce from a jar. It was Zach's favorite, with mushrooms and basil. *I know he'll like it,* she thought. They ate quietly, having given up on William, who appeared had been detained by some sort of official business.

"Don't wait supper for me," William had said, and after a long pause, he'd added, "Sarah, how are you feeling?" His voice had been eerily gentle and tired, and he'd sighed as he spoke. "We may need to talk later." She hadn't bothered to ask what about, diving perhaps into the protective possibility of an adulterous affair. William had indeed been spending an inordinate amount of time at the lab. This would give her something to think about—another chapter for a life in which she could dream herself abandoned and then vindicated or lost.

"This is very good" was all Manolo said, eating steadily while gazing at his dinner plate and looking up occasionally when ready to drink milk from his glass. He had recently stopped knowing how to make conversation when only Sarah was there. Over time, relations had become strained. She had assumed the habit of maintaining a tight silence, as if ready to implode for no discernable reason. To date, she had been a polite and solicitous hostess, but she had never taken him under her wing. Desiring no intrusions, she had systematically kept a distance. On this night, however, she noticed how hungry he was, and since William was not present to eat his share, she warmly offered it to an eager Manolo, who accepted with a proud gratitude. "Have some more. Go on." She shoveled another generous helping onto his plate before he could politely decline. He was not aware that Zach had gone missing, so he was surprised by Sarah's unseasonable softness. Had he known the reason for William's absence, he would have been just as surprised perhaps. During the meal, she persisted in monitoring his progress, ready to fill up his plate as soon as he had finished a helping, her smile warm and her gaze oddly loving.

When William returned much later that night, his clothes looked slept in. He had bags under eyes that appeared to stare into emptiness. Sarah did not see, because she lay in the dark. "I never noticed how helpful Manolo can be. He cleaned up after dinner, stacked the dishwasher, and swept up. He's quite a nice boy, you know," she said in a strangely cloying and sleepy voice before turning slowly toward the wall. When William touched her shoulder, she did not respond.

"They found Zach's car," he whispered. "I identified the luggage." Sarah lay without moving, stiff and impenetrable as a corpse. He was not altogether sure she had heard him. "I need to leave very early in the morning," he said quietly, as if to himself. "I'll be back when I can. Will you …" His words dissipated, as if into an empty room when one realized no one was there. He lay there until morning, staring at the window, illuminated from without by a waning moon and a light dusting of newly fallen snow. He puzzled at the randomly cascading folds of the curtains, wondering why they did not hang more evenly or why the folds were not equidistant from one another like lines on ruled paper. He did not hear her muffled dream whimpering, like that of a dog that had lost its master. She cried out in a tiny, barely discernable voice, as if from the inside of a telephone speaker held away from the ear. In the morning, when she found him gone, she vaguely and distantly presumed he was off on more official errands.

Although her headache kept her from work that day, it was not severe enough to prevent her from preparing pancakes for her guest. She was concerned that he never ate properly in the morning. She knew he would rush out, so she had the pancakes ready, buttered and spread but not dripping with the best maple syrup and covered in Saran wrap so that he could run and eat without soiling his clothes or smudging his fingers. He was surprised by this sudden demonstration of generosity. He grabbed the packet, uttered several abrupt thank-yous, and ran out the door. Sarah noticed how well Zach's shoes and hat seemed to fit Manolo. Was that Zach's shirt he was wearing as well? It had escaped her purview. She hadn't paid enough attention. In some far-off corner of her brain, she seemed to sense that Zach didn't need them right away. Why not let the boy avail himself of their offerings?

After he left, she noticed how many noises an empty house could make, from the aimless hum of a refrigerator to the creaking of heavy floorboards and the cracking of pipes carrying warmth to the extremities of a cold house. She recalled dreaming that she had been drowning in clam chowder with large chunks of unpeeled red potato and spongy white fish floating around her head. *We hang on the edges of sanity by a thread,* she thought.

When the phone rang at about ten o'clock, Sarah decided it was too early for unwarranted callers. She would take a couple of ibuprofen, return to the warmth of her down comforter, and sleep off the headache whose presence seemed more a distant menace than a reality of the morning. "Prevention is the best medicine," she told herself vehemently. A bit more sleep was all she required.

At midday, the aggressive ring of the phone awoke her again. In her state of late-morning drowsiness, she had heard it ring persistently several times. "I need some peace and quiet, for God's sake," she pleaded to no one in particular. She felt she had too many household chores to bother with annoying surveys or salesmen, so she decided to disconnect every phone in every room of the abundantly large house. This she did methodically, surveying each chamber for order and making a mental note of what had to be done to bring it into line. When she came to Zach's room, she opened the closet to seek out a piece of clothing he had recently worn. She found a sweater, which she quietly held to her face, sniffing for that faint, recognizable scent of a life she loved beyond reason.

Without removing her bedclothes, she started to straighten up her enormous house. She began ironing the shirts that had accumulated in the spare room. William normally did one shirt each morning before dressing. Today she would surprise him by showing him a closet full of neatly pressed shirts, each one draped on the same hanger as the trousers with which it would make an effective ensemble. She found herself wishing that William wore ties as well so that she could find him one for each combination she discerningly prepared. He would be surprised—she was certain of it. She struggled to suppress a giggle, like a child with a secret. Having finished with William's shirts, she descended the stairs to the basement and emptied the dryer of Manolo's clothing, carefully separating the shirts from other articles and bringing them up to the spare room, where she could continue the crusade for her family's personal order. Among her boarder's shirts, she found three she knew were her son's. She removed the three and lovingly pressed each into shape, applying mist first to the edges and seams. "I'm such a perfectionist," she said. "It is taking an inordinately long time to finish." She stopped intermittently and seemed to admire her handiwork. "My, my," she whispered to herself. When she had completed her task, she returned to the first three shirts for minor touch-ups. "Must be damp in the house," she reasoned, noting the shirts' inability to hold their stiffness. All this she did with a clear sense of purpose. When she suddenly sensed a terrible heaviness in her shoulders and lower back, she became confused. She sank to the floor and began gazing at the shape of her arms, noticing how the veins insinuated their way down through the backs of her hands into her fingers. With no particular wisdom to impart, they revealed only translucent skin surfaces bulging with blue rivers of life whose magnitude or brevity could not be measured by the eye, by instruments, or in time. As she attempted halfheartedly to see a movie with her mind's eye, she found the screen was a dull gray blank.

Sarah awoke with a start to find William lying next to her on their bed. His eyes—reddened from lack of sleep, she presumed—embraced her warmly while he held her right hand and patted it softly. She was surprised how much he seemed changed, and she wondered how she had not noticed it earlier. His thick, knotted, angry hair looked gray, submissive, and defeated. A tall man of generous proportions, he suddenly projected the fine-boned frailty associated with a man twenty years his senior—more shell than substance. How could she have failed to notice how old and fragile he had become? It was not important. She had to get on with the day's responsibilities. Sensing it was still early, she glanced at the radio clock's bright green digital time. New, modern, silent, verdant time carried its own aggressive explicitness—not like before, when clocks ticked and gentle chimes were reminders to savor the moment, to record the thought. Time, she mused, used to be colorless, like water or air. But now she must go.

Wrenching her hand away, she abruptly announced, "I need to prepare supper for Manolo. He'll be home very soon." Perhaps this feeling of lightheadedness came from not having eaten all day or that damned headache, which persisted despite all measures to the contrary. Perhaps her period would soon begin with a vengeance. It had been irregular of late, announcing itself with crippling headaches and arriving with heavy blood flows after absences of three months or more. Perimenopausal, they called it. But wasn't it too soon? She was still young. The price one paid for being a woman. "Fucking raging hormones." Wasn't it hard enough to stay afloat on even the good days?

Without a word, William watched her go and then closed his eyes. He saw her as she once had been; her black hair—now streaked with gray—was pulled back from her face, and her body was tall, lithe, light of step, and athletic, even when she went braless, which she often had before the baby was born. He appeared on the verge of saying something but then sank softly back into his pillow.

* * *

Manolo arrived at five o'clock in the afternoon with a girl of indeterminate age. She could have been anywhere from fifteen to thirty. She was voluptuous—with C or D cups for certain—but at the same time, she appeared innocent and sweet. When she spoke, Sarah recognized Beatriz from all of those annoying "I love you" messages she had left for Manolo. Manolo seemed a bit uncomfortable and mildly surprised to see Sarah still in her open bathrobe and nightgown. Her bare feet looked raw and dirty. Manolo found himself wondering why she had not worn slippers.

On a normal day, Sarah usually arrived home after he did. Her clothing gave him notice that she had not gone out today, and there was a sickly sourness to her appearance and smell.

To save Manolo the trouble of saying more than he needed to, Beatriz announced, "We are going to a restaurant together."

"Forgive me my appearance," Sarah apologized, as if she hadn't heard the girl. "I had a terrible headache, but now I feel better. Shall I make some spaghetti for you?" She noticed that Manolo was wearing Zach's canvas hat and running shoes. *How compatible the boys are,* she thought smiling to herself. Despite Sarah's morning sweetness and present eagerness to oblige even against his wishes, Manolo could not be certain if the seasons had changed or if he had recently encountered a gentle spell in the dead of a violent winter.

"Has Zach come back from the ski trip?" Manolo asked in his clipped, polite tone, suddenly recovered from temporary amazement.

"Yes. Would you like spaghetti or ziti or penne? With plain marinara sauce or with mushrooms and basil? I also have a meat sauce. Which would you prefer? Shall I make a quick salad and heat up some garlic bread?" She turned to Beatriz, who appeared confused by all of this frantic attention.

"Oh, really, nothing, please. We are celebrating with some classmates in a restaurant. One of our school friends is returning to Venezuela," she lied ambitiously in an English overburdened with heavy consonants.

By this time, Sarah had already set the pot of water to boil and opened a fresh jar of mushroom-and-basil sauce, Zach's favorite. She was moving through infinite space as if all other participants were frozen in time. She had seen it in a commercial once. Although she could hear their voices, she had trouble comprehending the sense of their words. For Sarah, it was still. If she could only keep it that way. Still, she felt as if she were inside the eye of a hurricane with the din of human voices swirling around her head. Did she recognize William's voice as well? *Words, words, words.* She had no sense of what they were saying. She needed stillness, sleep, and time to dream the next chapter. Had she turned the oven on? She carelessly slapped butter on bread, but where was the garlic? And the fucking press? *Why doesn't someone peel a clove for me?*

If she could have observed herself through the eye of a camera, she would have seen her surroundings completely out of focus, herself a rapidly moving picture superimposed on a blurred and incoherent background. The sink and stove were covered with utensils and pots, the table was strewn with the crude makings of tonight's dinner, and these faces, poised just on the periphery of focus, seemed all to turn and turn. She needed to boil water, add the pasta, heat the sauce, wash the vegetables for salad, mix up a fresh dressing, and spread the crushed garlic—she would never be done. She felt the kitchen spinning out of control. Suddenly, she heard herself gasping for breath. Then there was blackness.

* * *

When she opened her eyes, she was lying on the kitchen floor. She could taste the pasta sauce, which had spattered randomly in all directions. That its glass container remained intact while everything around it seemed shattered was one of those flaccid and insipid ironies that informed living and did more to amuse than enlighten. She sensed a dull ache in her head, her wrist seemed limp, and she could not lift it for the pain it caused her. William was holding her head up, and she noticed Zach standing motionless, looking down. She recognized his shirt and his shoes. She made a mental note to resew the missing button. She was calm again and mentally preparing to write the final chapter. With Zach there, her face brightened. "I'm glad you're all right. Do you realize how much you had us worried? Why didn't you call? Where were you?"

The stocky figure leaned over and gave her a bit of water to drink. "Sorry" he said in that clipped Castilian that had once but no longer sounded so peremptory. *Sorry* was suddenly the only word he could remember in that second language he had labored for so long to control.

For William too, the chapter had ended. He felt his resolute determination to speak openly to his wife about current matters abruptly deflate. His reasoned and cerebral approach to all events surrounding human behavior was suddenly exposed as dashed hope rather than truth and was as scattered as the sorry mushroom-and-basil tomato sauce upon the kitchen floor. For him, a long journey was about to begin.

* * *

As they walk back to the apartment with little Zach in hand, William notices that his wife has become calm and close like a sweltering room. "How could this have happened?" she keeps repeating under her breath. "How could this have happened?"

"That's life" is William's feeble reassurance.

Emerging suddenly from a world that has of late become increasingly protective, she shoots back violently without taking a breath, "What's life? Life is up and down, good and bad, life and death, love and hatred, courage and cowardice, black and white, loyalty and betrayal. When you tell me, 'That's life,' you tell me nothing." She stares down at the child, who is oblivious to everything except the cool sensation of chocolate ice cream on his tongue. She notices that the ice cream has melted in his hand and has flowed down along the side of his arm to his elbow like a sticky brown river of lava. She plans to bathe him in the evening so that he can sleep well. She intends to watch him while he sleeps.

"And you tell me everything," she whispers without looking up.

William strains under the weight of responsibility. "It's all in your choices," he answers. There is a hint of paternal smugness in his voice. He is tired to the bone. Yet he feels lucky: they have been spared. They continue to walk slowly back to the apartment.

Alcántara

We always seem to remember best those things we have lost, as if the mind insists on playing tricks on us, forcing us to recall events and individuals whom we labor to suppress. Shortly after she had married, Magnolia had bought a pewter shell in the form of a large abalone whose graceful curvatures she admired. *A five-dollar garage-sale bargain for an object of such refined beauty,* she had thought at the time. Having nowhere to display it, she had wrapped it thickly in newspaper and put it away in a closet until such time as she could give it a place of pride. When she and Peter had moved to a larger apartment, they had been forced to discard much of the junk they had accumulated in the early years, to which action the thickly wrapped gewgaw fell victim. By the time Magnolia remembered what she had abstracted, it was too late. She would always think of that pewter shell with a longing that accompanied the irretrievable loss of once-promising possibility.

But now her problems were those of an examined life. Magnolia had committed adultery with a man she had once believed to be her friend and spiritual equal. This notion did not need to be true—as if such things could ever be true anywhere but in books—for the weight of this perception to affect her frame of mind. In fact, the less true it was, the more distorted became her outlook, the more skewed her frame of reference. Once it became clear to her that the nature of the infatuation was ordinary, at least for him, she suffered a blow from which she would not recover. The acceptance of this loss, no matter how ill perceived, caused her hideous distortions with loved ones, who struggled to understand the abruptly changing ways of womanhood in the guise of wife and mother. It became, for her, like living with an old injury, a bruised bone. Although conscious of its presence as a defining event in her life, she was unaware of its power to wear her down. When there was a dampness in her mood, it was most often triggered by the recollection of events that had caused her to become frozen in a time beyond which she could not venture and from which she failed miserably to liberate herself. It was as if the memory of her failed association were richer than the relief afforded by forgetfulness. She lived with a residual sadness below the foundation of everyday melancholia. As she struggled to keep such memories locked inside, they acquired sinister force and made her difficult to be around.

* * *

They had driven up through Andalusia on highways vastly improved by twenty years of Socialist rule. Despite having effected a tremendously modernized infrastructure, the Socialists were thrown out for graft and rampant corruption. "But not before the roads were fixed." Peter, always the driver on these expeditions, repeated the phrase like a mantra each time he read another article about how low the Socialists had stooped. They had seen many towns along the way. In Baeza, they visited a medieval university of Andalusia, where graduating seniors had written their names on the stone walls in the blood of bulls.

"Quaint customs these Spaniards have." Magnolia was amused, while Lily scowled at the thought of those brutally murdered horned creatures rotting in the middle of the sweltering town square. There, they also had seen a statue of the wife of Hannibal. *And what was her claim to fame?* thought Magnolia. During the Spanish Civil War, a crazed anarchist, in a pique of mistaken identity, had blown off the statue's head, believing it to belong to a likeness of the blessed Virgin Mary. The locals had glued it back on and patched up the bullet holes.

In Granada, at the Alhambra, they had read about Boabdil, the last Moor driven out of Spain at the end of the fifteenth century. As he looked back upon his lost kingdom, his mother was rumored to have proclaimed, "Cry like a woman for the kingdom you could not defend as a man."

"Those were the days when men were men. Tough mother." Peter had thought of his own without much affection.

"Eez deeferent heere, no?" was Peter's attempt at Spanish burlesque. Although she believed his accent to be closer to that of a Mexican mariachi singer, Magnolia smiled, while Lily continued her bloody brooding.

* * *

It took another six hours through Extremadura to reach Alcántara, a town named for the oldest surviving specimen of a Roman bridge. Peter was preparing to teach a course on Emperor Trajan and Roman history of the second century AD, and he thought a few slides from the real thing would broaden his students' understanding and enrich his private thirst for the visual relics of dead civilizations. Although Peter was convinced, in his cynical posture, that his students could not care less in that local community college for the ascent and decline of cultures or for the ageless wonders of the ancient world, he tried to give them in a semester more than most were capable of absorbing in a year.

"I'm doing them a favor," he told Magnolia when they used the value of a European education as an excuse to argue.

"Give them a break, Peter," she implored. "All they want is to make love and earn money."

"So do I."

As he felt Magnolia slipping away from him, Peter retreated more and more into esoterica.

"I just want you to love me again," he implored dryly. The request had cost him dearly.

"Just give me time," was all she could muster.

In jungles of Byzantine knowledge, he felt distracted. The more tentative the relationship with his wife became, the more deeply he burrowed in the arcane passages of dead Latin historians, finding amusement in drunken palaver conceived and executed more than two thousand years ago.

Peter had been battered by a weakness of spirit. Lacking ambition and diminished by inertia, he had calmed his rapier tongue into submission and become a respectable family man. Respectable was not a label that resonated well with him. Magnolia had always understood he was a man of finer sensibilities who, in times of trouble, would turn his intelligence upon himself. Lately, he seemed disembodied, like a being uncomfortable in his own skin.

Once, long ago, when they had first met, he had made Magnolia laugh uncontrollably. "I'm only proper on the outside," he had said with a straight face. "But if you look hard enough, you will see in my eyes an inner playfulness." His mock seriousness had somehow charmed her. On one of their early expeditions through southern Spain, before Lily was born, he had pulled the car over to the side of a road next to a field of poppies in Andalusia to dance with her a classic bolero to the honeyed voice of Antonio Machín. A passing driver had leaned out of the car to shout some Latin pleasantry, which was eaten by the wind. Magnolia could still remember the ancient blue Citroën, with its open doors and windows, blasting radio music into a field of red flowers, and she wished she had understood what that motorist had said. Why, she wondered, after all of these years, did she remember wanting to know? It was with a smile that she still recalled these moments, despite the intervening years and Peter's ever-deepening bitterness, an acerbity that bordered on the morose even when he was not wisecracking. She hungered for joy—not just wit or comedy but joy that would cleave to her bones and penetrate her organs, leaving her breathless and excited, as in the old days. She wanted not just a temporary laugh or a mild chuckle but permanent bliss, unending beatitude.

* * *

Her mother's death a year earlier had left Magnolia painfully distressed. She suffered guilt because she should have done more and grief for all of the open questions that had remained unresolved between them. One always died only partly revealed, mostly undiscovered. Magnolia accepted such mysteries, and although all of this was true, there was more to it than what she publicly presented. Her mother's passing had left her with a nearly palpable sense of life's brevity, a feeling that she must embrace life in all of its possibilities before it was too late for her as well. With a sense of freedom strangely exhilarating and, at the same time, terrifying, she had embarked upon a madness of heart. When it had ended in what could be described only as emotional carnage, she had become a tad unhinged. "It amazes me that we are capable of loving others way out of proportion to their goodness or nobility of spirit or generosity of heart. How can we care so deeply for despicable cads and unrepentant rascals?" she had asked her counselor, knowing secretly that he had been neither. *It's what makes all of this so ambiguous,* she thought.

Esther, who wore florid print dresses and colorful shoes, did not indulge Magnolia in her sorrow. "Love is like a fly. It can settle on filet mignon as easily as on a dry, hard, sunbaked turd."

When Magnolia asked Esther why her lover had acted the way he had, she answered that she could only help Magnolia to understand herself. Esther, with liquid black eyes that contradicted her outlandish wardrobe, did not equivocate. "He played games. You practiced deception. Now get over it. 'Pull up your socks,' says the Indian philosopher Gokhalé. 'Grab an anchor.'" This was the only advice Esther would give. Magnolia struggled now for equanimity in the face of unrelenting feelings of grief—one public and the other private, one of deep loss and the other of secret humiliation—for composure and for the strength to resume the inexorable march toward responsibility.

* * *

Peter had hunted for a small hotel on the edge of the town square in Trujillo, birthplace of Pizarro. During the evenings, they would have a light supper at a local café and watch the Spaniards parade in their finery. It was their reward for long days of serious and exhaustive sightseeing. As late as eight or nine in the evening, the sun was still strong. Magnolia imagined them in an Italian movie, from behind dark glasses, watching others behind dark glasses, smoking cigarettes, and dreaming of sex. She wondered if adultery were a common occurrence in this small village where everybody knew everybody else. *I wonder what the consequences of being exposed are,* she thought. A Catholic church stood behind their hotel. She had heard its bells in the early morning while memories of what she now thought was fraudulent but exquisite lovemaking lingered on her subconscious. "Shouldn't things have meaning?" she asked herself, as if she expected an answer.

* * *

On the first evening in the town, they had sat out on the terrace, eating a medley of local cheese specialties. Manchego was Lily's favorite. Peter and Magnolia preferred the soft Cabral. While in Extremadura, they had learned to eat *boquerones*, small vinegar-bleached anchovies with olive oil and garlic. Shortly after the waiters had raised the canopy, a passing sparrow had landed droppings right in the middle of the table.

"A dead ringer." Peter had been amused. "A perfect bull's-eye."

"I'm not hungry anymore." Lily had scowled. "Can we order some more bread?" None of the food had been contaminated, but Lily had refused to eat another bite until more bread arrived.

"It's good luck, my mother used to say" had been Magnolia's wistful comment.

But Magnolia had hated Extremadura. She had found the heat unremitting and the local cuisine a bore. With detached curiosity, she had noticed that broom flowers proliferated under a merciless sun with little rainfall. She would make a point of buying some for her garden at home. This was certainly the border, a place beyond acceptable boundaries in her mind. Peter had explained that during the Spanish Civil War, Extremadura had distinguished itself for the violence of exchanges between neighbor and friend, brother and uncle, Republican and *Franquista. It is no wonder,* thought Magnolia, *if character defines destiny, then landscape shapes character.* In her eyes, the character certainly had influenced the cooking, which was bland and undistinguished on a good day. The local specialties, consisting of beef and mutton stews, she summarily dismissed as unimaginative and inedible.

"The food has no flavor! The mutton is boiled to death. Why don't they cut away the gristle? Why can't they import some *gambas*? Don't they ever eat fish here?"

Peter and Lily were forced into an alliance against the unpredictability of Magnolia's reactions. They found it a relief when she read or slept. Her alertness signaled danger.

For this reason, they often found themselves indulging in light suppers of bread and cheese in terrace restaurants overlooking a square full of strolling Spaniards. It provided distraction from the business of real human talk.

* * *

Lily's thirteen-year-old heart burned for all of the injustices of the world. She was still at the stage in life where she cried for injured and stranded animals, longed to caress puppies, and could be persuaded with pink frills and lollipops, yet she was beginning to change. Her face held the round, unfinished look that afflicted early teenagers just before their physiognomy began to shift. The cleft in her chin achieved softness in an expression that tended toward severity and judgment. Even at this age, she could pierce with a look. In her more sobering moments, Magnolia had speculated that much in Lily's appearance would depend on the events in the intervening years. If failure in love became preponderant, obdurate stubbornness would prevail. If, on the other hand, she were to find happiness, plump softness might dominate her features. Lily's look would always speak volumes, because she did not possess the capacity for subterfuge, as if she had not been granted a gene for survival dissembling. She was a child in whom hurt would cause the construction of increasingly elaborate shelters against the danger of emotional hurricanes—and the storms would be severe, for she was not a child of mild climates or gentle winds. But if she were lucky, Lily would try to save the world gently; unlucky, she would persist with a single-mindedness known to those who lacked moderation. Either way, by the time she became middle-aged, her response to the unfairness of the world would be the same: intransigent rectitude.

For the moment, she sulked in silence, her own private bee sting giving reason to mope. The swelling caused her considerable discomfort on the inside of her thigh, just below the line of her shorts, but for Lily, the pain was exacerbated by a child's sadness at the memory of the tiny creature's death throes after its unfortunate collision with her leg. She had watched it sputter and expire like a tired old engine after her screams forced the small Séat to the side of the old road and Peter had leaped to the rescue. He had brushed it out of the vehicle with an abrupt sweep and quickly extracted the stinger.

"Relax. You'll be okay. We'll get some salve at the next pharmacy."

"Why doesn't it fly away?" she whined.

"It's sick; it'll die. That's how nature works. Try to keep your feet inside the window from now on."

* * *

Magnolia was abruptly wrenched out of a dream. Coming to after drifting in and out of sleep, she registered the confusion and now began sluggishly trying to demonstrate more maternal concern, but her daughter's hysterics around the death of one miserable bee seemed to rub her the wrong way.

"Come on, Lily. We'll get some medicine when we stop."

"Don't need any medicine," Lily said with petulance. "Poor bee."

"Then don't let me hear any more about the bee sting, d'ya hear? Keep your feet inside the car, and we can at least take advantage of the air-conditioning. If not for my sake, then for your father's." Peter loved the country but hated the heat.

"But the new-car smell makes me sick."

"Look, Lily, you just can't have it both ways." When Magnolia piped up, her words always sounded peremptory and dictatorial to Lily. "With feet out, you take the chance of murdering more bees. With feet in, you're safe from breaking the creature commandments. I'm very sorry you don't like the new-car smell. There's a barf bag at the side of the door. Keep it handy."

"Creature commandments. What does she mean by that?" Lily mumbled under her breath. "Always saying confusing things, like she's smarter than everybody else. Bitch." She adored the use of her newly found profanity. She savored the secret power it implied.

Magnolia found her daughter's behavior over the top. With her own self-absorption, Magnolia was incapable of empathizing with the sensibilities of a gangling teenager who was becoming increasingly unfathomable and defiant.

* * *

Before being wrenched back into reality, Magnolia had hovered in an uneasy slumber in which she had dreamed of her mother. Levitating out of body above their heads, Magnolia had observed her mother and her lover playing poker in a smoke-filled room under a naked lightbulb. Their faces, illuminated by light, had divulged no clue as to the cards in their possession. *Play it close to the vest*, she thought, as she watched them in her dream. While Magnolia had struggled unsuccessfully to see their hands, she'd found it increasingly difficult to breathe, despite a sensation of hollowness. As she abruptly returned to the sluggish ambience of a Spanish summer day in a car without air-conditioning, she experienced only a residual ache that gave no hint of its origin. She deliberately thought again of Dahlia, who had asked for ice just before she died. She had been too weak even to lift her head from the pillow. Magnolia had wept while holding her hand and said how much she would miss her. Her mother had suffocated on gases emanating from deteriorating flesh—a common occurrence in such cases, she was told by the clinicians, nothing out of the ordinary. The extraordinary could only be experienced firsthand. The ordinary existed only in the telling by third parties. One more body succumbing to the effects of its own decaying was hardly a headline. The only thing unusual for the doctor was the name. "Flowers?"

Peter had spoken quietly to the attending physician. "A source of unequivocal pulchritude" was Peter's way of explaining the hopeful whim of an eccentric ancestor. "A tradition in my wife's family." Even sadness, for Peter, seemed cloaked in ire.

And so it was with her lover—a tawdry tale of adultery, a story she knew would be cheapened in the telling. "Nothing extraordinary in that." She could hear the voices. "Happens all the time. She should have known better." And she had, always believing that her tale of woe could have no happy ending. She had believed she would be damned no matter what she did. But instead, it was done to her—the abrupt acquittal, the gentle boot, mercifully. It was understandable but painful. It was the most-practical solution all around, really. No one was hurt, because no one knew—except for Magnolia, of course. "Do you expect me to deceive two people for something that means nothing?" she had asked the first time she detected ambivalence, doubt, or whatever it was that set her mind to thinking. The first time reason had tried to fight its way to the surface of her thoughts, she'd told herself that the sex had been wonderful. "No sex is casual," she'd told herself, hoping rather than believing it was true. It had felt like the perfect chemistry, like water finding its own level. And after? For far too long, she had dwelled in a state of confused longing and disappointment. Now that she was sure it was finished, she felt a sensation akin to relief. "I'm not capable," he had told her, "of what I think you want from this friendship." She hoped that with clarity, she could achieve peace.

There will be time to make repairs, she thought. *Time to pull up my socks.* The time of no happy ending had arrived.

* * *

The Bridge

Something magnificent and mysterious is a bridge. Britannica describes it as "a structure surmounting an obstacle such as a river or declivity." Arabic for "bridge," *al-Qantar-ah* stands for itself.

The bridge becomes visible as they turn down the old mountain road that has not yet been replaced by one of the Socialists' efficient highways. Now that they are out politically, no further improvements need be made. Not as glamorous a tourist stop, such as the Prado or the Guggenheim in Bilbao, Alcántara offers no seductive beckoning. Alcántara is, after all, the end of pilgrimage for stalwart pioneers— an insignificant station beyond borders, a stop at the end of the line. In fact, the road soon turns primitive as they approach their destination. So desolate and abandoned is the path upon which they find themselves that desiccated skins of small snakes and lizards can be seen among the pebbles that line their way. Lily notices a lizard scurrying gingerly out of harm's way and feels mild relief that it has managed to avoid being crushed by the tires. Peter explains that the bridge has been destroyed or damaged several times over several centuries and eventually rebuilt or repaired by any group that foresaw its usefulness. He launches into one of his short lectures. "The architect was so celebrated for his achievement that he was entombed nearby with the words 'I leave a bridge forever in the centuries of the world.'

"The arches can hold tremendous weight without mortar, without cement." He points out the keystone to Lily, who, for one fleeting moment, is lifted from her petulance.

Always the educator, thinks Magnolia, slightly amused that he needs to say anything at all.

He continues more for his own amusement than for the benefit of the two women. "It stands now as a proud testament to the art and architecture of survival." Peter is intent upon his own agenda, she is certain, seeking parallels and juxtapositions between then and now, noting similarities and differences. He will amuse himself by gathering perspectives, and perhaps somewhere, he will stumble upon a glimmer of naked truth. And if it jolts him, so be it.

* * *

As they pull into the small enclosure for cars, they read the plaque: "Puente de Alcántara, 106 DC. Arquitecto: Caius Julius Lacer." Peter finds the only shade available, next to two elderly Spaniards sitting in front of the monument to C. J. Lacer. Behind them is a small temple. "To Diana," Peter has already explained, "and next to it an original remnant of an old Roman road, Via Romana."

It is left to Magnolia to wonder and ask if it goes anywhere anymore. It appears they have arrived at a Roman dead end. The smaller of the two men stands and nods in greeting. His head bobs like a water-born apple, his nearly toothless gums masticating an unlit *puro*, a local Spanish weed oozing a brown molasses substance into the corners of his mouth while he speaks. Lily attempts not to stare but must fight back a repugnance that does not sit well with her compassion for creatures weak, small, and old. He volunteers to give Peter a short history of the bridge, and as he begins his narration, Peter notices that his dates and facts are not correct. The old man is probably looking for a tip to supplement his miserable pension, Peter reasons. It doesn't matter to Peter, who believes he knows more than is contained in any offering that some wizened old geezer with a moth-eaten *boina* could make. But on some level, Peter is looking for an excuse to give him his due, to make him feel that even in such a small endeavor as outwitting a foreigner out of a few *pesetas*, the old man is a success. Peter recoils at his own softness, which he perceives as weakness, but does not believe anyone will notice. His tone is formal and brusque. "*A ver*. Let's see," he says. Magnolia is too busy wondering how, on a day like this, the old crow can wear a black hat and a dark jacket over a shirt whose collar and sleeves are frightfully frayed, shabby, and gray.

* * *

Magnolia grabs her Nikon, which includes a zoom feature, a gift from Peter, and prepares to assess how to make the bridge most photogenic. She wishes to capture it from many angles. They have been riding for three hours without interruption, and the stretch does her good. She has left her handbag and all of her valuables locked in the car, which is clearly in sight. Instinct tells her there is nothing to threaten them here. The other old-timer has disappeared. Magnolia has forgotten he exists. Was there someone else as well? She should have been more attentive. Peter and the old man are hovering around the temple, examining Latin inscriptions. Magnolia laughs at the motion of the old man's buoyant black bean. *Must be a lot of wear and tear on that crow's neck of his.*

Lily has found a quiet spot in the shade to lick her wounds. Magnolia is certain the bee-sting episode still plays like a refrain in her mind. Each of us, she imagines, is off in a different direction, each of us lost in a unique vision of a superior world.

Magnolia makes her way slowly to the arch at the middle of the bridge. The air feels dry despite the presence of water. No breezes blow. The late-afternoon sun, though still daunting, is in retreat. The ancient stones of Alcántara are returning the favor, emanating the day's absorption of heat. As she moves, the seemingly hard pebbles crack and disintegrate under Magnolia's feet like tiny mirages whose existence has neither been questioned nor proven for centuries until the weight of a human foot reveals them to be figments of mind. There is no circulating air above the Tagus. It barely flows in the climate of this unforgiving land, which has been hauled kicking and screaming into the twenty-first century, leaving little of value behind, whether a rock, an ancient arch, or a temple to gods whose existence is relegated to footnotes in obscure academic journals. As she looks over the side, the once-mighty river looks more like a puddle, a swamp, a mere trickle. "The Roman army could cross without getting their feet wet," she says, chuckling. "All these happenings that alter the course of history look so puny to someone without an anchor. We are all condemned to oblivion, so shouldn't we live it up while we can?" For Magnolia, this is no cheap shot. "Perhaps with moralizing and lofty principles, we are too clever for ourselves by far. Life is so very short."

An occasional car makes its way across the bridge slowly. The predominant impression is of an abandoned miracle whose mystery has been wiped out by modern science. *Another instance of the extraordinary becoming commonplace,* she thinks. *Religion ceding its place to knowledge. And then, by its ability to survive the centuries, becoming extraordinary again.* But to Magnolia's eye, this bridge seems too powerful and proud to submit to the withering neglect of modernism. It appears to be pushing itself out of the earth, demanding attention, commanding respect. *More intellectual games,* she thinks. Condemned to oblivion, she repeats, "Pull up your socks." "But I'm wearing sandals." Life's senseless comedy, complete with the voice of an imagined poet dueling with his acolyte. A veritable cartoon flitters through her mind.

Whenever a vehicle passes, Magnolia turns to look at the plates, more to observe the country from where it is coming than the region. But only the locals are here. Rarely does she see a Spaniard from another province or even a Portuguese a mere six miles from his own border. The inhabitants of the few cars she notices seem comfortable in their air-conditioned interiors and display no intention to step out to admire one of history's masterpieces.

* * *

Lily's leg has begun to swell, and the itch is becoming unbearable in the spot where she was stung. She is examining it, when the old *boina* sidles up to her on the bench. They are not quite touching. Peter has heard all that he needs to from him and has vanished behind the Temple of Diana. Lily smiles and forgets her sting. She instinctively sits upright, trying to put a little more distance between herself and the old man's face. She is polite but has no desire for any interchange. Her incipient Spanish will not help her, she is sure, when he mutters things she cannot understand. His words slosh around brown saliva like oars slapping against water and then pass thinly through his nose, giving his speech a distinct liquid twang. "*Buenas dias*, senorita." He says it slowly with a smile. His oldness is repulsive to her, though she will not think it. Lily's eyes lock onto several large black spots at the base of his nose, which folds into his face like a flat, oblong serving plate. She cannot tell if they are moles or pores filled with years of unwashed discharge. She is so fascinated by the landscape of his face that she fails to notice at first that his eyes are not quite synchronized, as if a wire holding them together has been severed and each has rolled off in search of a different grail.

When he addresses her, she is not certain that she is the object of his focus and looks around to see if there is anyone behind her. She detects a strong odor of tobacco and decay, although she would be loath to call it that. He reminds Lily of a predatory bird in decline, blind and stupid, whose beak has been crushed by repeated collisions with the tree or the mountaintop he calls home. His head continues to bob like a rubber ball balanced on a spring.

"*Cuantos años tienes?*" he begins. She is trapped now.

"*Doce. No, no, trece.*" Perhaps this will be easy.

"*Te gusta mucho aquí?*"

"*Sí.*"

"*De dónde eres?*"

"*Sí.*"

"No, no. *De dónde?* Alemania? Francia?"

"*Sí.*"

"Francia? Sí?"

She has gotten it finally. His speech is different from the Spanish she has learned in language lab.

"No Francia. Estados Unidos. América." She pulls farther away and tries to look in the opposite direction. But she can smell his breath and feel it on her bare shoulder. Withdrawing to the edge of the bank, she realizes that shortly, there will be no seat left, but she is too shy and weak to get up and leave. She shrinks further into herself but makes no attempt to flee.

The little Spaniard's bouncing head performs its reconnaissance while continuing to chew his puro, and when it appears there is no one within earshot, he proceeds.

"*Ya tienes pelitos ahí abajo?*" His eyes, like two planes circling the runway, seem to come in for a landing on Lily's hands, which she has placed between her thighs while extending her legs. She senses something inappropriate. Little hairs below?

She has answered "Sí" before fully understanding the question. Her embarrassment is now plain as she attempts to move to where there is no seat left. *Where's Papa?* She instinctively imagines the man is an insignificant creature much like the emaciated homeless dogs wandering this countryside, and in her thoughts, something like pity is being replaced by fear.

"*Te gusta nadar?*" He speaks slowly, and his head protrudes closer to her as if trying to convey meaning to a companion whose hearing is damaged. Her eyes lock onto his unwashed pores, tiny dark ticks on the surface of the skin, which are close enough now to pluck. This repulsion gives her an outlandish sense of relief, as if she is dreaming—but only for a moment.

"*Sí.*" She has understood immediately. Her nervousness causes the answer to shoot out. There is a hesitation in her gaze. Perhaps she has misunderstood his intent. She relaxes for an instant, but her skin is still on guard.

"*Nadas bien?*" He persists.

"*Sí.*" She can move no farther away and is looking around for Peter. Although he appears intermittently, he has just moved behind the Temple of Diana again and is no longer in sight. She sees Magnolia watching them, she thinks, through the lens of her Nikon. But Magnolia then turns toward the water and focuses in another direction. Lily's terror is like a cold drizzle threatening deluge.

"*Yo conozco un sitio escondido en el río donde puedes nadar desnuda.*"

She has caught it. She has understood his intent even if her Spanish is insufficient to have captured every word. *Desnuda.* Naked. Although she is frozen, her mind has perversely registered feminine agreement in the use of the adjective ending in *a*. Suddenly, the little creature's open laugh reveals a mouth sparsely populated with dreadfully stained and neglected teeth. They smell. *He stinks. How does he manage to keep the puro aloft when his mouth is wide open? Where is Father?* There is no longer ambiguity in his questions.

"*Mi papá no me deja,*" she blurts out in perfect Spanish. She stands abruptly. Her voice assumes a higher pitch than is normal. She looks again in the direction of the temple to see if Peter has emerged from his explorations. She prays her mother will turn around one more time. She sees her watching through the lens again. She smiles brightly in the direction of the arch. She waves. "Hi, Mom!"

* * *

Magnolia has always kept her daughter in sight, although she recognizes the necessity for discretion. Lily will not countenance her mother's surveillance. Magnolia is too tired to undergo another row with her daughter. Perhaps they'll be able to talk about this trip to Alcántara in the future with pleasure. They'll remember it as one of the most interesting trips they have ever taken together—in the future, when they have healed.

When Lily looks up at her camera, Magnolia turns her zoom abruptly in the direction of the river. Lily's attempt to distance herself from the tiny man is clear in her body language. *Probably has bad breath*, thinks Magnolia. Lily, she is certain, would never show disrespect or intentionally cause embarrassment. *Better to suffer.* Believing her daughter to be in the presence of an ancient relic of a war she has only heard about, Magnolia retreats again to her own universe, until by some invisible compulsion, she is returned to an odd sense of her daughter's discomfort. She turns the camera again upon her daughter, who throws up her hand to wave as if to say hello with a face beaming uncustomary, alien friendliness. Magnolia turns abruptly and begins moving rapidly, not running so as not to set off any alarms, just determinedly walking in a brisk and intentional manner. There are a few hundred feet between them. "Lily, Lily," she whispers under her breath. "I'm coming, Lily. Mama's coming, baby. Wait." Magnolia waves her hand in reply. She wants to cry out, but her heart is beating too hard. "I'm coming, baby."

She crosses to the opposite side of the bridge, where she will not lose sight of her daughter for even one moment. By the time Magnolia has reached the midpoint, Peter has reemerged. Lily has run to him. "Daddy!" She knows now she is safe.

The old predator has ambled up to Peter. "*Es muy guapa, muy lista.*" His smiling, moronic expression briefly reminds Peter of a *Mad Magazine*'s octogenarian version of Alfred E. Newman. Although Lily is holding him too tightly, Peter looks nervously for Magnolia, and when he sees her approaching, relieved, he turns to the old creature. He mumbles a *gracias* for his help and hands him an unsolicited tip for services rendered—a donation for the elderly and perhaps the harmlessly insane. When Magnolia arrives, she is breathless. They turn and start moving in the direction of the car.

Magnolia stops directly in front of the old man's bobbing presence. She hears a wheezing as he sucks up air through his nostrils. His entire body is engaged in the labored task of breathing. He seems not long for this world, yet his jaw locks on the puro like a vise. His entire face insinuates into a smile, revealing again a few broken teeth, a cesspool of gums and tobacco, and an organic fag growing out of the crevices of his mouth. He holds up the five hundred pesetas handed to him by Peter and says, "*Muy guapa, muy lista.*" She suddenly finds herself trembling with what can only be described as rage—rage at the dying creature's predatory audacity.

"*Monstruo,*" she hisses. "*Sucio.*"

He smiles back at her as if he has not understood. Peter has returned, and with his arm around her waist, he is pulling Magnolia firmly toward the car. The old comedian's head continues to bob as he watches them go. "*Muy guapa, muy lista,*" he seems to be saying.

* * *

"Are you all right?" Magnolia has turned to look at her daughter in the backseat of the car. Her own hands are trembling, and the knuckles are bruised. Perhaps in her haste to reach Lily, she scraped them along the wall. She has no recollection of the camera banging from side to side against her rib cage. She does not notice the minor aches, which will manifest themselves later in skin discolorations. "Did he hurt you?"

The car is slowly pulling out. Lily can see the old man standing and waving good-bye. She notices that the other man has suddenly reemerged as if from nowhere and is coming up beside his compatriot, who is still waving the five hundred pesetas. Has he come from under the bridge? He too begins to wave. She does not return the gesture but continues to stare through the window.

"Lily, what happened?" Magnolia's frantic question intrudes on her daughter's reverie. Lily disregards her mother's inquisition, barely acknowledging the tone of terrified concern.

She does not look back at Magnolia. "Nothing."

Peter wants to hear no more of this. "Let it go."

* * *

La Mancha is flat and breathtaking in its austere simplicity. Its monotony makes it easy to read and to sleep, its sameness lulling one into a sense of peace and security. Peter says the Castilians elevated this nothingness to a virtue. *Nothingness?* Magnolia understands that he means simplicity, a lack of complication. Sometimes the landscape of shimmering wheat is broken up by a field of bright yellow sunflowers turning in unison in the direction of the sun or a lone windmill, a welcome anachronism in this land of smooth highways. There are hardly any cars on this *carretera* at four o'clock on a hot afternoon in the middle of Spain. When one passes, it is flying seemingly at the speed of light compared to Peter's sensible driving. Magnolia closes her eyes for a moment. *The rain in Spain falls mainly in the plain.* She can hear Rex Harrison's voice. Magnolia has tried to read, but she cannot. What happened to the days when she could read through anything—thunderstorms, TV, her parents' hushed battles from behind the bedroom door? Then she had read to stay alive, to keep out the intrusive reality of her parents' separation. Her father had left when she was about Lily's age. Magnolia had been too young then to understand what Dahlia had meant by "irreconcilable differences." For Magnolia, it had been profoundly personal and felt like betrayal. Magnolia could look back now and understand that he had been a good man, a warm and decent individual who was wounded deeply by her withdrawal. She had been shy around him whenever he returned, and after he remarried, she made no attempt to see him or to meet his new family. She doesn't remember her anger. She recalls, however, the compulsion to finish her books whenever it was time for a meeting with him, cutting short her visits and rushing away to discover the outcome of the novel—the reasons for the demise of a heroine, the identity of the murderer, the name of the perfidious thief, the wickedness of a scheming relative, and so on and so forth. Yes, he was a warm and decent person just trying to survive, like herself today, like Peter beside her, and like anyone whose soaring faith in life's endings has crash-landed on the rocks or become entangled in the blades of a lone windmill standing like an intruder in a vast field of serenity.

* * *

Lily is asleep now. The air-conditioning is on. Magnolia glances at Peter, who has been wondering how they will proceed from this point on and what they will do when they are home again. *Home again.* They have been driving in silence for several hours. She has no idea of their destination or any sense that she can discover significance in this odyssey. She has dreamed again and tells Peter so. In the dream, she is walking with him through a bright field of yellow sunflowers, when Dahlia taps her on the shoulder from behind. "Don't worry about me," she tells her daughter with a smile. "I'm happy now."

A Squirrel's Tale

It is still dark when he enters. I am luxuriating in a world between sleep and dream, which is pleasant for a change. When I open my eyes, I catch his look of terror.

"Mom," Jake whispers, "there's a squirrel in the driveway. It's dying."

Carlo turns. Used to waking at this time, he looks at the clock. He realizes it is Saturday and looks again at Jake. "Have you been out all night?"

Jake tiptoes around to Carlo's side of the bed. "Pop, there's a squirrel twitching right in front of the driveway." I don't understand why he is still whispering.

Carlo is about to close his eyes again. Like the unmistakable locking of a door with a dead bolt, the words hit their mark. "What?"

"Pop, there's a squirrel twitching right in front of the driveway." Perhaps because the bedroom is dark, Jake is still whispering.

"Do you know what time it is?" Carlo says.

"Pop, can you help me? I want to move it out of the way so it doesn't get hit by another car."

"Did you hit it?"

He hesitates. "No. It was lying there twitching when I got home. I had to swerve not to crush it."

There is a pause. I'm disabusing myself of the notion this is a dream. No matter what it is, I know I am not guilty.

"But do you understand, Pop? It's still alive. Can you help me move it?" His whisper has assumed an urgency that wasn't there when he first nudged my shoulder.

"That's just a reflex action. The squirrel is probably already dead."

Nice. Thank goodness for the voice of reason. Yes, Carlo. Thank you, I think, wanting to drift back into the dark demimonde without squirrels, rodents, snakes, or tree dwellers of any kind. There is a thread of something pleasant that I am struggling to regain, or perhaps I am guilty and curious. *Better,* I think, *to remain so, as none of us is innocent.* My comfort lends false integrity to such ramblings.

"No, it's not; it's trying to get up. It's moving its legs. You can see that it's badly hurt."

"Well, how do you expect to save it?" Carlo is the voice of reason again.

He will pluck me from the jaws of guilt if Jake manages to subside. *Down, boy.*

"Even if I can't save it ..." Jake has stopped whispering.

Now I'll never remember what trouble I was in unless I write it down. I don't wish to move yet, though I have returned to the land of cardboard smiles and plastic innocence. *Someone, give me a life-saving dose of prime-time TV, please, before I drown.*

Carlo, our Solomon, speaks again. "Call the animal-rescue league. They'll come out. They'll put it out of its misery."

Jake doesn't like Solomon's wisdom. He turns to me, the mother who, in a pinch, will always give him the answer he wants to hear, no matter how irrational or insane. With a twist to Solomon's wisdom, he says, "Mom, maybe they can save it or something." In a moment of waking sleep, he adds, "That's a good idea. Will they come out right away?"

"Call them and find out." I am awake now. I sense the storm clouds of another idiotic duty looming, large and not so silent. I have just traded guilt for responsibility. "Jake, it's Saturday morning. What time is it?" I look. "Fuck," I say under my breath.

By this time, I have hauled my still-warm body out from under the down and am peeking through the blinds. The creature is lying on its side next to the sharp, rounded granite of new pavement in a suburb of polite and discreet neighbors. There is movement. Whether it is merely stunned or mortally wounded, I cannot tell. For a moment, it appears to be trying to regain its equilibrium, straining with its front paws to stand upright. At the next, its head is down. I detect a gust of wind like a whisper, causing a slight spasm of undulating fur. *It would be Christian*, I think, *to remove it from the driveway tarmac and place it on the soft grass. It will not mind the morning frost.*

* * *

"Hello. There's a squirrel in my driveway. It looks as if it's still alive ... Uh-huh. Can you give me the number? ... Uh-huh. Thanks."

With all of the phones in this house, why does he choose the one right next to my bed? I have moved over so that he can sit comfortably.

With another number, he tries again. "Hello. There's a squirrel in my driveway. It looks as if it's still alive ... Okay, I'll call back in an hour."

Who said the SPCA never sleeps? Maybe they're out saving chipmunks or something. Better yet, they're dreaming of worlds without animal diseases, cares, cars, cages, or encumbrances of any kind. The operative word is *dreaming*. I'm feeling an empathic toothache coming on. My incisors are hurting. For a moment, I force myself to erase the picture of small rodent death from my mind. I remind myself that squirrels, when cornered, are nasty critters. So I have heard. What's one more or less in the world?

* * *

"They won't come out till eight. But in the meantime, it might get further gutted by another car. Pop, can you help me move it out of the way?" His voice is pitched for pleading. Jake knows I have trouble dealing with dead—or, in this case, dying—bodies. Solomon is on the roster again.

Solomon is recusing himself from further involvement. "Why don't you move it yourself?"

"Pop, it makes me feel uncomfortable."

I wonder if Jake's contriteness is his confession. *It's just a bloody squirrel,* I reassure him in my mind. He still has miles to go.

With a sigh, Carlo says, "Get a shovel out of the garage and ease it over."

"Pop, you don't understand."

"Do you know what time it is? I have no pants on," Solomon says.

No pants—reason must prevail.

"Just put some pants on. Pop, the squirrel is twitching." Plaintiff hope springs eternal.

"I have no shoes. It's six thirty in the morning, and you wake me up to tell me there's a dead squirrel in the driveway, and I need to perform heroic acts to resuscitate it? You want I should do CPR on a rat?"

"Listen, Pop. Just come help me. You're awake already. It'll take only a couple of minutes."

"Goddammit." Solomon curses the heavens. This song isn't over yet.

* * *

I have dozed again. My short slumber has dropped me before the junction of two gravel roads, leaving me with a feeling of dread. Carlo's side of the bed is cold. When I open my eyes, I see Jake staring at the floor. It seems he hasn't moved from my side of the bed.

"Mom, will you call the animal-rescue league at exactly eight and tell them to come over?"

"Jake, it's not seven o'clock yet. Since you're awake, just eat some breakfast. Then you can call them yourself." Is it possible that after all of this, I still believe I can find my way back to that fork in the road? Pernicious guilt or sweet innocence? Random firings or calculated targets for that gun-slinging id in me?

"Mom, the number is right there next to the phone. You'll be awake, won't you?"

"Geez, Jake, this is Saturday—my one day to sleep late. Where are you going now? To bed?" I cannot let myself get hysterical. *Get a hold of yourself. Where the fuck is Solomon? Did he find his pants? Something happened while I was searching for the fork in the road. Geography has morphed into a menacing weapon. It is now a real fork pointing at me.* "Hey, did I miss something? I thought your father was going to help you." I'm dreading that Saturday-morning headache.

"He's got an appointment to get the car serviced. He's getting ready."

"I see. So I'm the one. Jake, you come here at five thirty in the morning, singing me sad songs about a moribund squirrel, and then you expect your father and me to save it? Your father, of course, can't find his drawers and has more-important things to take care of. You're a young man. You drive, go to parties, and stay out all night. Why don't you just wait and call the SPCA yourself? I'm sorry for the squirrel, but I'm also tired, and I need to get some sleep."

"I can't believe what you're saying, Mom. The squirrel is twitching. Maybe it's just in shock."

"Then it'll come out of shock and walk away. It happens all the time on those wires." I am lying. I have no idea.

"Will it kill you to call them? The numbers are right next to the phone."

"Where will you be? Getting your beauty sleep, correct?" *A little too sharp on those* r's. *Tranquilla.* I mimic Carlo when he thinks I'm leaning too far into the gorge.

"I can't believe you have a problem with this. Yeah, I'll stay up, but if you're going to be up anyway," he doesn't finish the sentence. "I can't believe you'd balk at doing this little thing. Such a thing!" That's how he utters frustration.

"Such a thing!" I repeat. *Eyes on the prize.* I suddenly have a vision of him pinned against a wall by one hundred pounds of water from a fire hose with a couple of German shepherds nipping at the seat of his pants. *Ugly picture.* It comes easily to an unquiet mind. "Such a thing." I am sitting up now. I have abandoned any hope of finding that fork which has now morphed again into a giant pitchfork in my mind. My eyes are wide open, and they are flaming. Carlo has found his pants and created a sparkling ensemble with shirt and shoes. It occurs to me suddenly that I could turn this episode into one of those flatulent personal essays I hear on NPR. *Suburban housewife, nothing to do, saves squirrel to the admiring ears of thousands of public-radio listeners.* The truth is no one gives a flying fuck about houses of strangers undermined and brought down by tiny termites, rodents, and other incidentals that assail their foundations day in and day out, come rain or come shine.

"Are you two going to have a battle about this now? Jake, you need therapy. Just wait an hour and call." Carlo is grabbing his wallet. He is on his way out.

"Jake, why don't you ask your father to call?" *A slam dunk,* I think in my delirium. Father is in the room, dressed and ready. I'm practically naked, elsewhere, looking for a piece of monster cutlery in my brain, and the edge of a thread of a faint possibility of revelation.

"He helped me to move it. He's leaving now to take the car for a tune-up."

I suddenly relax. "Where did you put the squirrel?"

"Under the tree."

"What tree? We don't have a tree." Maybe I *have* found that pitchfork; maybe I'm being impaled by it. I mustn't be awake yet.

"The next-door neighbor's tree."

My next-door neighbor is an old lady whose constant companion is an oxygen tank. "What! You put a dead squirrel on my neighbor's lawn?" I'm cool. "That's just great." Morning light is burning off the fog. I haven't found the pitchfork. The pitchfork has found me.

"Under the tree, it's protected."

"Why didn't you put it on our lawn?"

"We were afraid the cats and birds might attack it."

"But under the neighbor's tree, it is better camouflaged, right?" Where the hell was Solomon when this was decided? I do not pursue this line of inquiry. "There's an old lady who lives there. What if she comes out to get her newspaper and sees the squirrel twitching under her nose? She might just keel over. Baby, we're looking at a potential lawsuit. Maybe even manslaughter."

"I can't believe what I'm hearing. You don't care about the squirrel. You're worrying what the neighbors will think in this happy ole suburb. Such a thing."

There he goes again. I sense disdain for my bourgeois propriety, but I'm undaunted. I forge ahead, full throttle. "Well, yeah. It's not customary for people to deposit carcasses on their neighbors' property. At least not in America. In Afghanistan maybe. Or Islamabad for sure. But not in Pleasantville. Why don't you just go pee on the neighbor's lawn whenever you need to relieve yourself?" It's an honest question.

"You both need therapy. I'm going to the garage." Solomon's superior wisdom strikes again. He has no patience for suburban soap operas with bad actors and inane plots.

"Why don't you call since you're so smart?" *Hey, Sol, where you going? When are you coming back?* As usual, there is no answer. *Stop thinking now, Sol, and answer me.* I feel my ears turning incandescent.

"So, Mom, will you call at eight?"

My eyes are now wide open. I look at my firstborn. His eyes are crossing. He hasn't slept at all. He has tried to save a noisome pest in the best way he can. *He's a good boy,* I think. *Kept young by indulgence and protection.* We're a happy family again. The pain of the pitchfork hasn't quite receded into the cauldron. It'll be back soon.

"I can't believe you two have deposited a soon-to-be-dead squirrel on my elderly neighbor's lawn and are leaving me to pick up the pieces and sweep up the mess. Thanks, Son." The mouth is faster than the brain. Although I say it, I am calmer now. I am a mother first and a combatant second.

"And I can't believe you are so worried about what the neighbors think."

"Okay, I'm leaving," Carlo says from downstairs. I didn't realize Solomon was still on the premises.

"I thought you'd escaped from this asylum." *Gone for the day,* I think. *Again. Leaving me peripheral. Like an output printer. Activate when necessary. Peripheral devices have inner lives too. Just ask me.* "Hey!" I shout. "Who wants to know what I am thinking? I dreamed I just murdered someone—cut his throat with dull scissors." I seem to be screaming, when I hear the front door slam. Is that a smile spreading across Jake's face?

I utter a heartfelt "Shit."

Jake is laughing uncontrollably. "I'm going to bed, Mom."

"I thought you were worried about the injured squirrel on my neighbor's lawn. Why didn't you ring the bell and put it just inside her door, where it would be better protected from predators?" *The smoking gun again.*

Jake is laughing so hard now that he is doubled up on my bed. The bed heaves like a tsunami while he throws himself from side to side, gasping for air. This continues for longer than I can fathom. I am not watching the clock, but I'm sure that enough time has gone by to swim the channel or paddle a canoe across Lake Erie.

"Thanks, Mom," he manages barely.

About the Author

T. Agvanian has always been interested in the history of World War II in Russia and other former Soviet Republics. She earned a degree in Russian Literature and History. She currently lives in Massachusetts with her family. This is her first book.

Printed in the United States
By Bookmasters